THE HOSTAGE

SURVIVE!

THE HOSTAGE

By Larry Weinberg

Grosset & Dunlap
New York

Cover illustration by Chris Cocozza

Text copyright © 1994 by Larry Weinberg. Cover illustration copyright © 1994
by Chris Cocozza. All rights reserved. Published by Grosset & Dunlap,
Inc., which is a member of The Putnam & Grosset Group, New York.
GROSSET & DUNLAP is a trademark of Grosset & Dunlap, Inc.
Published simultaneously in Canada. Printed in the U.S.A.
Library of Congress Catalog Card Number: 93-70037
ISBN 0-448-40433-8   A B C D E F G H I J

To Michael,
my marvelous adventuring son —L.W.

His mind had been in a black hole; for how long he didn't know. And when he finally became conscious again he was coughing and choking and lying facedown in a pool of water. Desperately, he tried to push away from it—but he couldn't get his hands free from behind his back. He started to lift himself up, and realized that he couldn't see. Someone had dropped a hood over his head. He needed to breathe, but there was only a tiny opening at the mouth of the hood. Greedily, he started to gulp air through it, but there was hardly any time. The rubbery bottom of a huge boot came crashing down on his neck and head—and drove him back into the water.

He started to panic. He didn't even know where he was, except that he must be in a boat. Mingling in his ears with the pounding of his own heart was the soft *put-put-put* of a motor and the humming of wooden planks under his face.

But now his mind started working furiously. Would he be heard if he screamed? *Should* he scream? Would whoever had kidnapped him kill him if he moved or made a noise? But if he stayed on the floor, he'd drown for sure in just a few inches of water.

He was getting ready to risk lifting his head again when someone grabbed him by the jaw. "I wouldn't try that, me lad," a man with an Irish accent whispered in his ear. Strong hands then turned him on his side, and a thick rag was shoved under his head. "Breathe," murmured the Irishman. "But don't yer say nothin' 'til yer told. If yer understand me, nod yer head."

He nodded, but he was still groggy. It was as if sleep didn't want to let go of him. Thick clouds were swirling in his brain, making him dizzy. His head felt like a swelling balloon that was ready to explode, and he was afraid that he might pass out again.

Breathe! he commanded himself fiercely. And lying there with his lips pressed against the opening in the hood, Paul Spire sucked in the hot damp air of the Amazon jungle.

Now that he was conscious, he could think about what had happened. It came back in flashes: the burst of gunfire passing over the open Jeep he'd been riding in; looking back to see a van closing in behind him and a dark man leaning out of a side window firing an automatic rifle into the air; Paul's driver muttering a prayer in Portuguese and shoving his foot down on the gas; the little Jeep bouncing wildly over the thick and twisted roots that kept blocking the narrow dirt track; the jungle on one side, river on the other; monkeys and crocodiles scurrying away, but for himself and the man behind the wheel, no escape . . . no escape at all.

The driver had turned to Paul suddenly, his face covered with sweat. "I am sorry," he said hurriedly in broken English, "but I am poor man with big family and I think maybe they don't want *me.*"

The Jeep jolted to a stop, and the driver dove straight from his seat into the bush. Paul watched him, wide-eyed, as he scrambled to his feet and began to run. But the van also came to a halt, and the dark man with the rifle jumped out after him. Though built like a tank, he was fast. Paul heard his thick boots smashing through the undergrowth. Seconds later there was another burst of gunfire—and a loud scream of fear and agony. Then silence.

This had all happened so fast that Paul hadn't thought of making a run for it. Now a man almost as thin as a skeleton—and wearing, of all things, a New York Mets baseball cap—was coming toward him. But he carried no gun! Paul jumped from the Jeep, his eyes darting this way and that—to the jungle, to the river, then back again.

But it was too late. The driver of the van, a red-headed man, stepped out with a rifle at his side and shook his head in warning.

In an instant, the skinny man had taken Paul by the shoulders, spun him around, and pressed a wet rag into his face. The last thing that had passed through his reeling mind as he tried to keep from going under was that the smell of the rag reminded him somehow of hospitals . . . and people dying.

As the boat moved on, Paul heard a whirring and grinding noise that he somehow recognized. He thought for a moment and then he knew. It was coming from the gigantic hi-tech sawmill at the widest part of the river. He remembered the driver of his Jeep pointing it out shortly after picking him up at the airport. It had been brought in parts all the way from Japan, then reassembled here in the middle of the jungle.

Well, if they were passing it, he reasoned, then they must be going upriver. And probably they were traveling on the far side of it to keep away from the barges and those great rafts of floating logs he'd seen coming downstream, blocking the river by the sawmill. He remembered noticing that the small boats going in either direction on the river had been crowded together to avoid those barges. Maybe one of them would be coming close!

Sure enough, it wasn't long before he heard voices and snatches of guitar music floating over the water. As the sounds drew nearer, the men in his own boat began to stir. He thought again about crying out for help. But then he felt the boot—and a sharp prick through his hood. It was the point of a knife pressing into his Adam's apple. He nodded carefully to show that he understood, and the knife was pulled away. Now he began to smell some kind of alcohol, and the men around him started to laugh and shout drunkenly.

Some men in a passing boat called to them in a kidding way as their crafts drew near to each other. Except for the Irishman, they all traded loud jokes in Portuguese. Then the second boat moved along and the men in Paul's boat started acting sober again.

"Keep behavin' yerself, boyo," the Irishman said a little later on. "And in a few hours we'll take the hood off yer."

It seemed like forever until that finally happened. But when the Irishman slipped the hood off Paul's head, he left him tied up at the bottom of the boat. And before the boy could manage to lift himself up far enough to see over the side, his eyes were suddenly covered again, this time by a piece of cloth. The Irishman bent down close to him. "Sorry lad," he whispered. "At least yer can breathe better now. Best I can do for awhile."

Paul settled back, trying to forget how helpless and frightened he was—trying to forget he was even there at all. He felt the boat slow down and heard the engine die out. Rough hands picked him up and pushed him out of the boat. Paul stumbled blindly until the Irishman grabbed his shoulder to steady him. He untied the ropes around Paul's wrists and pulled off the blindfold.

Paul blinked in the sunlight. In front of him was the boat, bobbing gently in the water. A heavyset man, the one who had killed Paul's driver, grinned through broken teeth and tossed a banana to Paul. It was green, but he ate it anyway. Paul decided to call this burly man the Tank.

Even when he couldn't see, Paul had known he was traveling in an open boat. And it hadn't been hard to figure out from the leak and the smell of rotting wood that it was an old one. He'd lived almost half of his fourteen years on Cape Cod with his grandparents, surrounded by boats. From the sound of this one he'd guessed it had an old-fashioned outboard motor with the tiller at the stern. And he was right. The motor had been turned off and was tilted up to keep it from scraping the bottom of the stream. Somewhere along the way they had branched off from the main river onto a smaller one. Now they were stopped along the shady shore, taking a break before moving on.

The Irishman lit a cigar that looked like a twisted bit of black rope, and jerked it at a flat chunk of rock close to the water. "Yer must have some business to do by now, boyo. Yer can step over there."

Paul gave the area a worried look and the Irishman grinned. "The crocs and snakes are over on the sunny side."

"Is it okay if I go behind that tree?"

"Suit yerself," said the Irishman. "But I wouldn't touch nothin' yer don't look at first."

The moment he was out of sight, Paul

dipped into his jeans pocket and brought out the letter from his parents. The driver had handed it to him at the airport, but he'd simply stuffed it away. He hadn't wanted to read whatever their excuse was for not meeting him after he'd been flying for sixteen hours in three planes. It was because of all their other broken promises that he hadn't wanted to come visit them down here in the first place. How many times had they written to ask him to be "understanding just one more time?" Well, that time had ended with a bang when they didn't even come home for his grandpa's funeral! But Paul was hoping now to find out why these men had kidnapped him and murdered his driver—and maybe the letter would give him a clue. It wasn't as if the Spires were rich enough to pay any kind of a ransom. All they had was the small salary they got from the environmental organization that supported their work to save the rain forest.

He tore open the envelope. "Paul dearest," his mother had written. "This is a terrible way to greet you, I know! But your dad and I have to stay at our outpost. I can't explain why in this note. Orlando will bring you here. Oh, we just can't wait to see you!"

He crumpled the note and tossed it away. It told him nothing. Not a thing! And as for their being so anxious to see him, they sure had shown *that* often enough! Going back to the boat, he knelt by the water's edge to rinse his hands.

"Wouldn't do that," said the Irishman, whom Paul nicknamed Red. "Water's too muddy here to see what's comin' at you. Might be some of them little devils in there."

"Devils?"

The skinny man with the bony face of a skeleton gave a hollow little laugh. "Piranha!" He wheezed and began to cough.

Paul swallowed hard. He'd learned about those deadly fish in school. They could eat the flesh off a body within minutes.

Red noticed the frightened look on Paul's face. "That's right, boyo, be scared." The Irishman chuckled as he got back into the boat. "Yer won't find no mercy in the jungle."

They stayed close to the shady side of the river as they went along. Even so, the Irishman would watch the sky and listen carefully. At the first sign of a plane he'd glide the boat out of sight under branches until they could go on unnoticed again.

After several hours of this, the boat turned into the mouth of a smaller stream. Even where there was open sky overhead, the river seemed dark.

The Irishman seemed to read Paul's mind. "Do yer know why that is, lad?"

"No."

"Yer mean yer folks is biologists an' all that and they didn't tell yer?"

Paul didn't answer.

"It's because all these floatin' leaves and the vegetation in here sucks up so much of the sunlight, boyo."

In the front, the Skeleton made a motion for silence. The Irishman nodded grimly and turned off the motor. Then, laying their rifles across their knees, the men reached for paddles.

"Mind you, no noise from here on," Paul was softly told. "Sounds travel easy over water and we're comin' up to Indian land."

He'd been given a paddle of his own and he was glad for something to do. Paul had always loved the water. Dipping into it calmed him, and the steadiness of the effort helped drive away some of his fear of these men. They kept at it until a breeze sprang up. It was the first break in all this heat, but to Paul's surprise, the others stopped paddling, and the Irishman brought them to shore under some trees. Quickly the men spread out a roll of plastic tarp, then tied the corners to the lowest branches above their heads.

Paul was bewildered. He looked up at an afternoon sky that was still bright and clear. Why were they in such a hurry to stop and make camp? The answer came moments later when the black clouds rolled in over-head and cracked wide open.

Having lived near a beach since he was seven, Paul had seen some terrific summer downpours. But he could just imagine being back in school and telling about *this* one. "You would have thought you were right under Niagara Falls," he'd say. And crouch-ing with the others beneath the tarp, the boy could almost pretend to himself that he and these three murderers were all good friends stuck in the rain together. He shook his head politely when the Tank passed a bottle of a fiery kind of rum called *kachasa* to Red, who took a swig from it, then offered it to Paul.

The Skeleton in the Mets cap had a bottle of his own. His eyes gleamed like hot coals as he drank from it. But his chest heaved silently and fired off jerking little coughs. He tried to stifle his coughing in a dirty rag, and his eyes streamed with tears from the effort. Yet that didn't stop him from gulping the raw and burning alcohol.

Less than an hour later, the storm was over. The late afternoon sun came out again, but the men seemed worn out. There was time now to drape mosquito netting over themselves. It was still very hot but, to the boy's amazement, they all put on heavy clothing. Then the Skeleton and the Tank fell asleep where they squatted, leaving Red to take the first watch.

Paul let his mind drift. Soon he was filled with worry and fear. Escape looked impossible now. It was probably a joke even to think about it. He should save his strength and get some sleep like the others. But he couldn't help listening to the flying bugs attacking the netting. And it made him itch all over just to hear them.

Then in the pitch-darkness of night came the bats. He had always liked these creatures. He enjoyed hearing about their caves and how they were guided by a kind of sonar. But there was something weird about these particular bats that reminded him of the Dracula movies. They seemed to be hovering just outside the netting, even walking around their little camp, as if wondering how to get at the men. Paul had been scratching at his arm and he'd even drawn a little blood. All of a sudden one of the bats lunged at him. Its ferocious jaws ripped right into fabric only inches from his uncovered arm, and Paul cried out.

Whap! Red's backhanded slap caught him across the top of his head. "Them vampires won't make yer bleed to death," the Irishman muttered angrily. "But some Indian's blow dart sure as hell will if yer don't shut yer yap."

Softening a bit, he said, "Here, put these on. It's harder for them to bite through these." He tossed the boy a thick woolen shirt and a scarf.

Paul lay awake for most of the night before drifting off. He was dreaming about fishing with his grandpa when it seemed as if a thousand whistles went off at once.

And they had. Small green birds by the hundreds darted in front of his face. And when they cleared away, he noticed that the Skeleton was standing on the shore coughing up yellowish globs. He held the baseball cap to his mouth and was spitting the globs into it. The other men were watching as he rubbed the disgusting mess into the fabric, then carefully set it down on the end of a branch. Then he backed away from it and climbed into the boat, his eyes glittering strangely. He grinned like a crazy person.

Paul waited until they were on their way upriver again. Then he quietly asked Red what that was about. But the Irishman seemed embarrassed and looked away.

As the long morning hours went by, Paul began to notice that the stream was changing. Fewer and fewer fish swam in it. And at places where water flowed over rock, he could see a strange yellowish shine. But it was the change in the jungle around them that amazed him. The great umbrella of leaves that had been overhead all this way was gone. The trees had all been destroyed somehow. In their place he saw small, twisted, stunted plants—and stumps of what had once been a forest.

The farther they went, the more the plants thinned out. There was no soil on the ground, just cracked reddish clay or patches of rock. No birds flew here. No snakes drooped from branches or slithered into the water. No monkeys jabbered at the travelers. No animals came down to the waterside to drink. No half-submerged crocodiles slid past them disguised as logs. There even seemed to be fewer insects circling in the air. And the heat! Without shade, it was like being scorched by the bottom of a hot steam-iron.

But the men in the boat seemed more relaxed. There were no Indians around to worry them. And the signs of civilization that they saw—little farmyards and wooden shacks—didn't worry them either. The shacks had collapsed long ago. The farms were abandoned and in ruins.

The Irishman cocked an eye at Paul. "Can you explain this to us, lad? You being the son of such famous scientific parents, I mean."

Paul bristled. He didn't say anything.

"No, I can see that yer can't. Well, then, I'll explain it. First the logging company came in. All the grand old trees, the ones yer can make expensive furniture with, well they got cut down. Then the poor farmers was let in, hungry for land. The farmers, well they cleared away the wood that the loggers didn't want by burnin' it. That's a good way to fertilize yer crops, you see, with ashes. So the crops grew fer a few years, but then the earth give out. That's because there's never been much soil at all under all those grand trees. The trees protected the soil too, from the sun. But now the sun beats down and down and down. No more crops, no more soil. And even the trees will never grow back. It's a desert." Red lit up a cigar. "No charge fer the lesson. Just thought I'd keep yer informed."

"I already knew that," Paul mumbled.

"Oh did you now?" Red replied with a slow grin. Paul looked away in anger.

The shores farther on were lined with abandoned metal pans and long, shallow wooden basins about waist high through which water might have been passed.

"There was gold here once," the Irishman explained without being asked. "Big nuggets that came down off the Andes in some great flood who knows when. Got a few men rich years ago, but a lot more of 'em dead. Sometimes it was guns and knives that did them in, but mostly it was all that mercury, boyo—the damned chemical they use to clean up the gold. Ruined my friend Claudio here." He pointed his cigar at the Skeleton. "He was a big strong man like Araujo there. But when he lost his resistance to disease, tuberculosis got him."

"Why did he spit all that stuff into his cap and leave it behind back there?"

The Irishman sighed. "Ever since he took an arrow in his leg, Claudio's had it in for Indians. The arrow was poisoned, but he lived. Now he poisons them back. Nothing'll kill an Indian quicker than a white man's germs."

Paul was stunned. "But if you knew that why didn't you stop him?"

"Me?" The Irishman took a long draw upon his cigar, then shrugged. "As long as he does his job right, everything else is his business. I didn't make this world."

"But you *live* in it."

The Irishman blinked under the boy's stare and looked away, grumbling. "Well I'm still around, if that's what you mean. But only because I stopped tryin' to change it. Now don't get me angry, boyo. In your situation that don't make no sense at all."

The loud throb of an engine broke the stillness of the ghost camp. With a whoop of joy, the Tank pointed at the sky. "El Senhor!" he said happily. And he lifted his liquor bottle in a toast to the descending helicopter.

"Don't tell me something actually happens on time around here," Red muttered to himself as the green-colored Huey settled out of sight behind a concrete shack. Paul saw that there was a landing strip behind the shed, like a little airport in the middle of the jungle. But then without warning, Red dropped the hood over Paul's head.

"It's fer yer own good, me lad. If yer to stand any chance of gettin' out of this alive, then yer don't want to show the Senhor you've seen what he looks like."

Five minutes later they were flying. He heard the Senhor's voice just once. "Put the boy out."

Paul smelled the rag soaked in chloroform before it was jammed under his hood. "Don't fight it. Let it work on yer," whispered the Irishman.

But Paul did fight it, secretly. Perhaps they hadn't poured enough of the liquid on the cloth. Or maybe there was enough fresh air seeping through the mouth-hole to help him resist. He wanted to hear what the Irishman was saying about him to the Senhor.

"I know yer don't pay me to think," Paul heard Red say, "but I've been studying this boy. And I can see clearly that the kid is not the first concern of his mother and father. They've put him behind them a long time ago. Yer can tell that from how he doesn't know hardly anything about the work that

they do. And that's very strange, 'cause he
seems a bright lad. Either they hardly write
to him, or more likely, he's so angry with
them that he hates their work and puts out
of his mind whatever they say about it. What
I'm trying to say is, yer dealin' with fanatics
here. To people like that a bit of suffering
and dying is all a part of how noble they are.
Yer see what I'm sayin'? Now I'll do anything
yer tell me, of course. But the way I see it
now, the more we do to the boy the more we
only get their backs up. So I don't know, I
leave it up to yer."

There was a long silence while Paul and
the Irishman waited together for the
Senhor's answer. But the chloroform fumes
were seeping into the boy's head. He held
out as long as he could. Then back he slid
into that deep, deep black hole.

When Paul came out of his drugged sleep he heard snoring around him. It was nighttime, and when his eyes grew used to the gloom, he saw that he was in a little cabin. He lay on a mat on the floor. The three men who had captured him swung from hammocks tucked away behind mosquito netting.

He thought that they might not have expected him to wake up yet. And maybe he wouldn't have if swarms of pesky insects hadn't stung him awake. But now he could just barely make out a little light shining through a crack in the door. And it seemed that if he could just get to the door quietly enough, he could walk right through it!

He was still wearing his sneakers, still in his clothes. Silently he drew his knees up under him, pushed down with his hands and rose. Then, crouching low, he carefully put out a foot to test the wooden floor before shifting all his weight to it. Not a sound! Good. He took another step. Then another and another, past the sleeping men.

On a hook beside the door hung the water canteen he'd seen being used in the boat. He lifted it off slowly and put the strap over his left shoulder. There was no handle on the rickety door. He put a hand against it and carefully pushed.

It creaked! The sound was really no louder than the chirp of a mouse. But to Paul it was like a firecracker going off. He bit his lip and stopped moving.

Not daring even to breathe now, he listened hard. The Irishman and the Tank were still snoring away. And the Skeleton's mucus-filled throat rattled with tiny explosions that sounded like a train engine trying to get started. Paul timed the spaces between them. One, two, *cough*. One, two, *cough*. He waited for the next, then pushed the door all the way. Its creak was buried under the sharp sound of the cough—giving Paul a second to rush out of the shack.

Was he really free? There was no road anywhere. Just a clearing in front of the cabin, then darkness beyond. Peering into the blackness he began to make out trees, towering trees. Paul turned around. On the other side of the cabin were the same great hulking shapes. But there the trees seemed to grow on some sort of incline.

Suddenly Paul realized that this land wasn't flat like the part of the rain forest where he'd been taken hostage. This was a mountainside!

So where was he? Was it possible to escape? He couldn't stay with these kidnappers—they might kill him! But then Paul tuned into the noises around him. He wasn't just hearing insects now, but *animals* crying out in the dark. The terrible sounds of the rain forest filled his ears, holding him back. But he couldn't be frightened—this might be his only chance for escape. He *had* to go.

With his heart pounding, he started for the trees. But then he saw *eyes*. Eyes and nothing more. They were large and round. There was a shine to them that couldn't have been a reflection of the moon—because there was no moon. The eyes were very still. They did not blink. And they were staring at him.

He remembered his dad had said once that in the jungle you don't stare at an animal. If you do, it might be taken as a signal that you're going to attack. So why was this thing, whatever it was, staring at him? Was it going to attack?

Paul felt his knees go weak. What chance did he have out here without a weapon? None at all! He'd have to sneak back into the cabin. He'd have to get something he could use to fight with. A kitchen knife, maybe. Or even one of the guns.

Moving silently to the door, he listened at the crack. Nothing had changed. They were still sleeping. He waited for another cough and slipped back inside. Now he could see much better in the dark than before. A semi-automatic rifle, an AK-47, lay propped against a wall not far from the door. Paul had seen how its safety catch was released when they were paddling up the river where Indians lived.

As he lifted the gun, he realized that these three kidnappers were now in his hands. All he had to do was let loose on them. Didn't they deserve it for killing the Jeep driver?

And what kind of people would want to kill off Indians by deliberately making them sick? If he got rid of them, he could just wait here until the Senhor came back with his helicopter and then *make* the man fly him back!

Carefully he picked up the gun, waited for another cough, and flipped the catch. Why were his hands shaking? He ordered himself to calm down. He could do it. Sure he could do it! He was strong. He was powerful. He'd just have to pretend he was Rambo—and *do it*.

He brought the gun into firing position and turned toward the hammocks.

"How old are yer, lad?" the Irishman asked quietly.

Paul jumped back, sputtering, "Four . . . fourteen."

"I was a year older than yer when I killed me first man in Belfast for the IRA. Been on the run ever since. But yer, God love yer, they'll probably give yer a medal for doin' such a noble deed to rascals like us."

The boy tensed and the arm that held the barrel began to tremble. The Irishman sat up behind his netting, lit a cigar, and waited.

What's wrong with me? Paul thought. *This is my chance! Why don't I shoot?*

"So yer going to finish us? Or yer going to put it away and get some sleep?"

He felt defeated. Ashamed. He was so disgusted that he almost thought he deserved whatever was going to happen to him now. Slowly he lowered the gun and set it down against the wall.

"Right choice, lad. But fer the wrong reason. The clip is out of it."

Paul went back to the mat and sank down. Quietly, he began to cry.

He had no idea when he'd fallen asleep, but it was the delicious smell of green bananas frying in cinnamon and oil that awakened him in the morning. The Irishman waved him over to the table, but as he started to get up, the Tank and the Skeleton began to snigger.

"Why are they laughing at me?"

"Nothing, lad. Don't pay them any mind."

"But I want to know."

Red pointed to the Tank. "Araujo here says that when yer had a chance to run for it last night yer let a porcupine scare yer out of yer pants."

Roaring with laughter, the Tank stepped away from the wood stove. "I like you, leetle girl," he said with a big wink and started toward Paul.

Paul sprang back to the wall, yelling, "What does he want?"

"Careful," warned the Irishman. "If yer get him mad I can't help yer."

But when Araujo closed in, his breath stinking like a corpse, Paul's arms flew up to cover himself. The grinning man brushed them aside as if they were a couple of twigs. Then opening a hand as large as a bear's paw, he pinched the boy on the cheek.

While this was going on, the Skeleton had been turning the dial on a battery-operated shortwave radio. He'd been getting static, bursts of music, voices in different languages. But now there was a woman speaking in English, saying, "My husband and I haven't heard yet from whoever kidnapped our son."

"That's my mother!" Paul cried, ducking away from the Tank, his face burning.

Mrs. Spire had paused to let an interpreter translate her words into Portuguese. Now she continued. "We are not rich. We have very little money. But we'll do whatever we can and we pray for Paul's life and that he won't be hurt. Please, whoever you are, contact us!"

The news announcer took over, speaking Portuguese, but this time there was a background noise. To Paul it sounded like the roar of a machine. The broadcaster was asking questions of a man named General Roberto DaCosta. And as Paul listened to DaCosta talking, his eyes opened wide with amazement. *That* was the voice he'd heard in the helicopter, ordering the Irishman to "put the boy out." The *general* was the Senhor!

He stared at the faces of the men around him. They were smiling! And why shouldn't they be happy when the man in charge of catching them was their own leader?

The Skeleton turned off the radio, the Tank dished out the food, and they all sat down to eat. All but Paul. He'd awakened starving, but now that he knew how small his chances of being rescued were, he had no stomach for anything. Going back to the mat, he lay there telling himself over and over, *I should have run last night! I should have run!*

The hours after that passed slowly. Red had gone back to his hammock and was reading from a paperback book. The other two sat at the table taking fiery gulps of *kachasa* and playing cards. Paul soon noticed a chattering sound outside. Confused, he looked out the window. There was a little monkey in a cage outside, making frantic noises and banging on the bars of its prison.

Paul walked over to Red. "What's going on with that monkey?" he asked.

"Don't ask me, lad," Red said without looking up from his book. "Yer don't want to know. They captured it this mornin'."

The Skeleton and the Tank just gave Paul a long, hard look. No one was smiling or winking at him now. Paul could sense a growing danger. And finally the Skeleton, reaching down to a leather sheath on his leg, pulled out a dagger and slowly ran a finger over the edge. Then he held his finger to the light so Paul could see it bleed.

Paul felt like he had to do something to break up this tense mood. But what? Anything, like talk. Propping himself on an elbow, he turned to the Irishman in the hammock. "Is it all right if I call you Red?"

"Call me anything you like," he said. "But it won't help yer to try making a friend of me, if that's what yer up to."

"No, I . . . I was just . . . uh . . . wondering if you came down here right after you killed that man back in Ireland."

"Here?" Red repeated. "Still being clever with me, are yer, boyo? Want to find out where *here* is, do yer?"

"What I meant was coming down to the Amazon."

"Took me some years before that," Red said and turned a page. "First I roamed around a bit."

"Where to?"

"Not going to let me read, are you?"

"Just wondering where you went."

Red looked up. "Why anywheres there was an uprising of the poor and the oppressed against their masters, don't yer know. Oh I was a great believer in all sorts of good causes then. Let there be a liberation movement somewhere, and there I was, in the thick of it, getting meself shot at."

"But what happened to you?"

"Yer mean, boyo, why did I change?" Red gave a bitter little laugh. "Because me comrades and meself always ended up the same way—dead or being tortured in prison or turning ourselves into ordinary bandits. So I wised up to just going after the money in the first place. It's money, don't yer see, that makes the world go around. And it's them that has the money who always win out in the end."

"But I don't get it!" Paul shouted in frustration. "You heard my mother say we don't have any money!"

"Ah, but there's people who do have it. People that don't much like how yer parents stop them from making a lot more of the stuff. The Amazon is still rich, boyo. There's still wealth of all kinds in it. But that's harder to get at right now because the World Bank has stopped lending money for new roads and such like. And why? Because there's these do-gooders who keep sending back reports about how the jungle is beginning to die."

"But you were showing me that yourself! It's the truth!"

"Oh the truth, is it?" Red said sourly. "Well maybe so. But shall I tell yer an even bigger truth? The one gigantic truth that runs the world? Money has to be made, no matter what! And these folks of yours are bad fer business."

"Then what do you want them to do? Change their reports? Give up their work?"

Red sat up and gave him a look that was almost gentle. "What yer really want to know is the chances of us letting yer go when we're done with yer. Well, if it were up to me I might do it, even though yer know what I look like. But it's worse luck for yer that yer found out who the Senhor is."

"Who is he? I don't know!"

"Yer lying," Red said grimly. He snapped his book shut so hard that it sounded like a pistol going off. "Yer should have kept a poker face when yer recognized his voice on the radio. We all saw it."

Getting up quickly, he went straight to a shelf. When he turned around again, he had a Camcorder in his hands that he aimed at the boy. That was a signal to the others, and the Tank pounced. Dragging the startled boy to his feet, he shoved him to the table, where the Skeleton stood waiting with his knife.

"Sorry, lad," mumbled Red, as the recorder taped the growing terror on the boy's face.

"But right now yer going to lose yer thumb. The boss wants us to show we mean business, one finger a day."

Ignoring Paul's screams, the Tank grabbed his right wrist and forced the clenched fist to the table. The Skeleton coughed excitedly. His eyes were gleaming now as he clutched his knife.

"Better open the hand or he'll cut it all off," Red said quietly as he squinted into the eyepiece. He sounded distant and ashamed. "Claudio's a bit crazy. Don't wait 'til he gets out of control!"

But Paul wrestled, yanked, kicked back. He couldn't break the Tank's powerful grip, and now he had to fight to keep from fainting.

"Red listen, please listen!" he gasped. "I haven't done anything to you. Not even when I thought I could use the gun!"

"Spread yer fingers, fer God's sake, lad. Spread 'em!"

"I . . . I can't!" stammered Paul. "I . . . I'm trying. I can't open my hand!"

"Be still, leetle girl," the Tank breathed in his ear. "Your good friend Araujo will do it for you." One by one he pried open the fingers.

Red gave a disgusted look at the Skeleton, whose weaving knife was now performing a little dance over the boy's outstretched hand. "Get the bloody thing over with, yer sicko!"

The Skeleton glared at him, then lifted the knife high over the boy's twitching thumb.

It all happened in an instant. The blade streaked down. But Red threw himself against the Skeleton's arm. The knife caught the tip of Paul's thumbnail, scraped the skin . . . and sliced into the table.

Hissing and coughing at the same time, the enraged Skeleton pulled the quivering blade free and swung it at the Irishman. Blocking the slash with the Camcorder, Red tried to duck back for a weapon of his own.

It was just then that the helicopter's roar filled the cabin. With a last murderous glance at Red, the Skeleton sheathed his knife and went out. The Tank let go of the sagging boy and followed after him.

"Thank you," Paul mumbled shakily. He steadied himself against the table.

"Save it," snapped Red, going for the hood. "Now I've got to put yer in this. It's for yer own good. If me partners don't give away that yer know who the Senhor is maybe he'll let yer live a little longer. That's the best I can do fer yer. Now stay put and say nothing."

Anxious minutes passed as Paul waited to know what his fate would be. Now he heard footsteps outside. Someone was entering the cabin alone. The footsteps stopped. He could sense that he was being looked at, studied. The silence was terrible. Then he heard the deep voice of the Senhor.

"She who is your mother," he began slowly, "does not know the place of a woman. He who is your father does not know the place of a foreigner. They have not the right to tell *us* what to do in our own country with *our* lands, *our* Indians, *our* resources. The reasons they give for this meddling we do not believe. We know what the real reasons are. Your country does not want us to develop and grow strong. The United States does not want any other nation to have wealth and power in the Americas but itself. This is what your mother and father are trying to do to my beloved land."

The Senhor paused to let his anger die down. "Of course I do not blame *you*," he continued. "I feel pity for you, boy, in my heart. But it is your own mother and father, not I, who will bring destruction down upon you. This is their punishment for seeking to harm us. But to show that I am a human being, I will listen to you if you wish to beg for your life. Do so now."

Paul started to open his mouth, but he could find no words.

"Why do you not speak, boy?"

Not knowing what to say that could help him, Paul just let the words fly out. "You're wrong about my mother and father. They do what they believe in, no matter what. No matter what." He stopped for a moment. Wasn't this what Red had said about them in the helicopter? But Paul didn't mean it that same way! No! Paul meant it in a *good* way! Even though they didn't come to his grandpa's funeral. Even though . . .

"And . . . and killing me won't stop them," he plunged on. "It'll only make them fight harder."

"You may well be right." The Senhor

sighed. "Perhaps they *are* simply fanatics."

"No, they're not fanatics!" shouted Paul. "And they aren't trying to make your country weak. They're trying to help the world be a good place for everyone!"

"You speak as a child speaks, I am afraid," the Senhor said. "Foolishly, but with a pure heart. And with a loyalty that I admire."

Paul heard the men go out and the helicopter lift off. Then Red came in by himself saying, "I have to hand it to yer, boyo. Yer pretty good at pushing a man's buttons. He's changed his mind about yer fingers coming off. But Claudio told him yer know who he is. So there will be a day or two more of filming yer alive and whole. But then . . ."

"Then what?"

"Yer figure it out," Red said, removing the hood.

Paul's mind began to race and he sneaked a look at the Irishman's wristwatch. It was a quarter past two. In a couple of hours the heavy rains would start. And maybe the Senhor had to beat them out getting back home. Taking a chance he asked point blank, "How fast do helicopters go?"

"It's about 150 miles to where yer have to go," Red answered slowly as he went to his hammock. "But even if yer knew which way, it would seem more like a thousand. Besides, yer don't have water purifying pills. Yer don't have a way to make fire. Yer don't have no weapon. Yer don't even have boots to keep the coral snakes from biting yer. Yer don't know nothing in general about surviving. And we would hunt yer down in no time."

"So I don't have a chance, is that it?" Paul snapped back bitterly.

The other men were returning. Red leaned back on his pillow, saying, "If that's what yer think, yer already good as dead." Then he closed his eyes.

———

Paul felt as if he were alone, even though the Tank and the Skeleton were sitting in the little cabin with him. For almost two hours they sat at the table, drinking in silence. So far they had ignored him and the fight with Red had been put aside. But they were in a bad mood anyway.

Red, meanwhile, had begun acting

strangely. His eyes were still closed, but he talked to himself under his breath and kept shifting around as if he couldn't get comfortable. Suddenly, his lids popped wide open, and he bounced out of the hammock. Grabbing a pack off the floor, he returned to the hanging bed and dumped out all his belongings. "Damn it!" he shouted. "Where are me bloody quinine pills?"

Paul sat up. "Want me to help you look?"

"No, and don't butter me up, kid! Won't do yer no good! Now where the bloody devil is that bottle?" Lurching into the center of the cabin, Red began looking everywhere. His search grew wilder by the second. He had begun to tremble now. And with a burst of curses he finally called out to the others for help.

The Tank only shrugged his shoulders. The Skeleton did get up, but he had something else on his mind. He went to his rifle, brought it back and calmly began to clean it.

Staggering back to the hammock, Red knocked all his belongings to the floor. Then he threw himself onto the hammock, shuddering.

The other two men ignored him. The Skeleton took a six-foot piece of rope from a peg. He and the Tank went outside to the monkey cage. They managed to get the rope around the frightened creature's neck. Then they pulled the monkey from the cage and tied it to a stake in the clearing.

"What are they doing to the monkey?"

Red didn't answer. His teeth were beginning to chatter. And the creases of his forehead and face ran with little rivers of sweat.

"Let me get you some water."

Red could barely get the words out. "G . . . g . . . get away from me! Do as I say!"

Paul stepped back just before the others returned. With hardly a look in Red's direction, the men moved the table away from the window and took down the plastic that covered it. Then crouching out of sight with their guns, they took up firing positions. The Tank and the Skeleton were too interested in what they were doing to notice Paul coming up behind them. The monkey was chattering furiously, pulling on the rope. One of the low hanging branches at the rain forest's edge had begun to dip. Something unseen was moving along it. Now a large catlike form appeared among the green ferns. It was a jaguar!

It pounced on the terrified monkey, ready to tear it to pieces. The men stood up and fired a single shot apiece.

Blood spurted from the jaguar's side. A cry of pain and savage rage rose from its throat. It wheeled around and bolted back into the forest.

The Tank raced from the cabin, shouting curses because they had failed to kill it. The Skeleton started after him, but turned at the door to glance at Red, shuddering in his hammock, and then at Paul.

There was another length of rope on the peg. Rapidly tying the boy's hands behind his back, he lashed the rope to a rafter overhead and ran out again.

Paul was helpless. But as soon as the Skeleton left, the Irishman swung around in his hammock. He was still shaking, but not as badly as a moment earlier. His bare feet dropped down and he half fell to the floor. Then, knowing exactly where to look for the missing pills, his trembling hand went into one of his boots and plucked out a little bottle. After stuffing two of them in his mouth, he dragged himself up.

"Why are you doing this for me?" Paul asked, as Red's fumbling hands went to work on the knots.

"I'm *not* doing it. Yer wasn't tied good enough and did it yerself. Head downslope. That's east. Then follow the flow of the rivers. But mind the sky for the 'copter later on. Cause if I see yer I'll have to kill yer. Now put me back in me hammock. Grab what you can fast and get out. It's a thousand to one a boy like yer will make it out of the jungle alive. Five hundred if yer act like a man."

An ammo clip and a cigarette lighter lay among Red's other belongings scattered under the hammock. Moving at a mad pace, Paul snatched them up, and slammed the clip into Red's gun. He'd need some food, too. From a jar in the kitchen area he pulled out strips of beef jerky and stuffed his pockets. He also grabbed the water canteen and rain poncho.

"Thanks for saving my life!" he called from

the door, but stopped when Red raised himself up on the hammock.

"The b-boots, yer dumbo," he stuttered. "Take me boots."

This time he was too excited and too relieved to be afraid of plunging into the jungle. He heard the hunters' guns going off ahead and to the left. Good. He turned right.

It was impossible to keep from stumbling as he ran—or *tried* to run—through a tangled mass of vines that hugged the ground like a sea of barbed wire.

Reaching out for something to keep himself from falling, he remembered too late Red saying, "Don't touch nothing yer don't look at first." His fingers closed around the thick spine of a flowering plant. He pulled back, yowling, as its thorns punctured his hand. Then he stopped for a moment in terror. Could the hunters be close enough to have heard him? Maybe not, but he had flushed out a wild turkey. The scrawny bird bounced away faster than he'd thought any turkey could go and buried itself in the high bushes.

Paul had even more reason than that startled bird to get away from there quickly. But he was no thin-legged fowl who could just hop on through that tangled sea of creepers. They tugged at his pant legs and scratched through the socks above the ankles. And his sneakers had soaked up so much mud from the heavy rains that his feet slid around inside of them as if the shoes had magically grown three sizes too large.

"Go downslope," Red had said. That was east. But the ground didn't slope in any particular direction here. It rose and fell over rocks covered by mossy patches of earth. Without the downslope, he'd need to see the sun to figure out which way was east. All he needed was just one large opening in all those leaves high overhead and he'd be able to tell where east was. But the great canopy covered everything. It was a greenish twilight down here, like being a hundred feet under water.

Paul went on and on without knowing where he was going or being able to keep track of what half-turns he had made coming 'round the giant trees. For all he knew he could have been going in a circle.

He was soaked with sweat, and hot from carrying the rain poncho. And Red's boots sure weren't doing him any good if they weren't on his feet.

There was a log nearby. Giving it a once-over first for anything that seemed dangerous, he sat down, slipped off his Nikes, tied the lace ends to each other, and strung them around his neck.

He was just getting the second boot on when he heard a crunching sound. The log, which was practically hollow, gave way under him. Before he could get up, he felt ants running up under his jeans and down into his boots. By the time he was on his feet the invaders were rushing up to his stomach, his chest, his throat.

These weren't back-home garden-type ants. They didn't tickle him, didn't make him itch. They were much too busy biting into his skin with the fury of demons. They were white killer ants, and in no time at all he felt like his body was on fire! Paul ran like crazy, slapping at them wildly. But he didn't have enough hands to kill them all—and meanwhile he ran without knowing where to run. He staggered over creepers and mounds of earth that turned out to be the homes of red-colored ants. In his panic, he thought that they might start waging war over who owned his body! There was a patch of daylight showing through the trees ahead—and the sound of rushing water. He scrambled toward it and broke into the open.

The dying jaguar lifted its spotted head, tongue and whiskers coated with its own blood. The great cat had been hunkered down on a branch that dipped into the swiftly moving stream, trying to lick clean its wounds. But now it saw an enemy like the ones who'd shot it. Snarling as it gathered its strength for one last fight, it arched up, set to leap.

As Paul sprang back something happened inside of him. There was no fear, just a kind of explosion of light in his head. He was raising the gun though his arms felt numb and sluggish. And even as he fired, he knew that he did not want to kill. Oh lord, he didn't want to kill anything—even this half-dead cat!

But Paul did kill, though he fired high. There was a squeal, not from the jaguar but something smaller. He heard a tiny crash in the leaves high above, then a closer one and another. Finally a small silvery animal—was it a squirrel?—there was no head!—hit the water. When Paul looked away from the river, he saw that the cat was gone.

It took but a moment before those maddening bites broke through his numbness. As he started to rush toward the stream he heard thrashing sounds behind him. Whirling around, Paul saw the glint of one gun barrel, then two. It was the Tank and the Skeleton!

Slinging his own rifle over his shoulder, Paul frantically waded into the water. It was slippery going over the loose, slime-covered rocks on the bottom. But there were long branches jutting out over the narrow stream. With no time to worry about what he might be grabbing hold of, Paul pulled himself along with the branches. But about midway across, he looked back and saw the Tank bursting out of the rain forest. Then the Skeleton ran out too, firing away.

Paul let go of the overhang and slid backward into the current. As it carried him away, he lost all control over what was happening to him. Luckily, the water was deepest here. No sharp rocks jutted up high enough to crack him wide open. The gunfire rattled overhead and pinged the water around him.

The watercourse swerved around a bend, taking him out of range of the gunfire. But now the stream was giving up its zigzag course downhill. It was speeding up, heading for a plunge. And Paul could hardly keep his head above water.

Desperately, he tried to get a foothold somewhere. But he was swept along, moving too fast to grab hold of any outcropping from the shore. With a last effort, he managed to lift the rifle overhead. It was only a few inches above him, but the strap caught on a branch. The jolt was terrific, and nearly pulled his arms out of joint.

Paul lost his hold on the rifle and was carried away, but not far. The snagging had slowed him and given him a chance to twist sideways. Now he reached for another branch and pulled himself to it. Seconds later, he saw his rifle float by. He grabbed for it, but missed.

Paul sat on the branch, breathing hard. He ached all over. The gun was gone. The rain poncho, too. But then, so were the stinging ants.

Now what? He could try to catch up with his gun. And it probably made sense anyway to follow the stream. "Take the downslope," Red had said. "That's east. That's the way to go."

But what about the two men? Were they still chasing him? He tried to listen for them above the sound of the water as he picked his way along the shore. There was little to hear except some squawking far overhead. And from the trees nearby came the high-pitched shrill of some smaller birds.

After a while something began to trouble him. There was something unnatural about a couple of the birdcalls. Stopping to concentrate, Paul waited for them to come again. There they were. The louder one came from behind him. The lower one did also, but from across the stream. If the two men were coming down the river on both sides of him, they'd be signaling each other. Wouldn't they?

A desperate hope came into his mind that maybe these were only birds after all. Maybe those two guys thought they'd killed him back there. Or maybe they'd just figured he'd never make it through the jungle anyway. He forced himself to stand still for a few more minutes and keep listening until he heard the warbles again. This time he was sure they were closer.

For a moment his legs were too shaky for him to do anything. Then he exploded into movement. Paul bolted into the rain forest, plunging deeper and deeper into the foliage until he was far from the stream.

But the same birdcalls showed up again on either side of him. And then coughs. Human-sounding coughs. The Skeleton's coughs!

"Leetle girl," the Tank called from another direction in a jeering voice. "We take you back. We don't hurt you, leetle girl. No, no. We like you v-e-r-y much, leetle girl."

It was growing darker, getting harder and

harder to see where he was going. The only way to make out shapes now was when the fireflies flickered in front of him. Meanwhile, Paul's trackers were also having trouble. They'd gone after the jaguar while it was still daylight, when they hadn't needed flashlights. They were using cigarette lighters now. That helped Paul. They couldn't see him, but he could see them. And the Skeleton's coughing was getting worse. The night air seemed to be making him sicker. He began to shout at the Tank, who just grumbled and swore.

After a while the little flares went out. Then the coughing was gone. The taunting and the cursing too. The only sounds he heard now were made by insects. It was as if the two men had vanished.

He wondered if they'd turned back. He remembered how the Skeleton had bit down on a rag to stifle his cough so the Indians wouldn't hear them. Maybe the men were trying to sneak up on him.

But Paul couldn't just wait for that to happen. By the dim and flickering light of the fireflies, he trudged on.

Then his toe nudged something that moved. Suddenly there was a thud against his right boot just above his ankle. And—*thwap, thwap*—two more!

Pulling away, he made out the dark rising head of a snake. Its needle fangs hadn't been able to punch through the leather. But now the recoiling snake was aiming higher.

Falling back out of its range, Paul tripped—and once again broke the rule about grabbing what he hadn't looked at first. Groping for anything that could steady him, he brushed against a branch and touched something alive and scaly. Oh! Another snake?

Croak! A little tree frog dropped to the ground and skittered away.

Perhaps it was instinct, or maybe it was just his desire to get away from the snake that made Paul think of climbing up onto a branch. Once he had done it, he reached up and climbed another. Then higher.

Now he was beginning to smell something very familiar. He thought for a moment and then realized that it was the scent of urine.

As if to tell him how right he was, a troop

of monkeys began chattering at him from the limb above. Then he heard dripping sounds. Pattering sounds. More urine!

It dawned on him that they were warning him away. It was their way of saying, *This tree is ours! Keep off!*

He stopped where he was—and the monkeys stopped too. Then he thought, *Hey, if it keeps me away from them, maybe I can keep other animals away from me.*

So, rising up on the branch, Paul took a lesson from the monkeys and peed in a wide circle on the leaves below him.

Then, snuggling up against the trunk, he wrapped himself in his own arms and shut his eyes. The air was pretty clear up here. But it wouldn't have mattered. Not even squadrons of flying bugs could have kept him awake.

The rain forest had its own alarm clocks. Piha birds went off like screeching teapots. Howler monkeys lived up to their name. Bright blue and yellow macaws squawked from their perches. And the air around the sleeping boy vibrated with the tiny flapping wings of hundreds of hummingbirds, green as emeralds.

Paul rubbed his sticky eyelids, sneezed once or twice, and reminded himself that he was curled up in a tree.

His first thoughts were of his parents. That came as a surprise to him because he usually didn't think much about them. Or at least he used to try very hard not to. Now he found himself missing them. And it wasn't just because he was scared.

Maybe it was because of the way his mom's voice sounded on the radio yesterday. She'd sounded as if . . . well . . . like nothing could be more important to her and to his dad than his safety.

Paul realized he was getting teary-eyed. *Better cut it out!* he told himself. Crying was definitely not his thing, and hadn't been for a long time. Besides, he'd suddenly remembered what Red had told the Senhor in the helicopter about his folks. "The kid is not the first concern of his mother and father. They've put him behind them a long time ago. . . . We're dealin' with fanatics here."

Well, maybe Red had to say that! Paul thought as he tried to shake off the heavy feeling that was weighing on his chest. Sure, that was just Red's trying to stop his boss from having him killed. And if the Irishman were here right now, Paul would explain to him that the reason his folks didn't take him with them years ago was because of his health. He'd been sickly, with allergies and colds and all kinds of stuff.

No time for this, Paul thought. *Got to get a move on!* Leaning over the branch, he made sure nothing dangerous was moving around below. Then he sat up a bit, letting his legs dangle over the side, and stared at the rain forest around him. The foliage was so thick that he couldn't see very far in any direction.

It occurred to him that maybe he should check out his belongings before doing anything else. He already knew, of course, that the gun, his only weapon, was gone. That was for starters. The poncho, too—another big fat terrific. But at least he still had the canteen he had taken from Red, although it had been banged around. Lifting it, he found that most of the water inside was gone. Great, just great. He looked for the leak and at first couldn't find it. That was partly because it was caked with dirt—and partly because it was a really small puncture, like the kind that took hours to let all the air out of the tire of a bike. The damp spot he found after wiping it clean was the tip-off. And luckily it wasn't at the bottom. Paul wondered if he still had that pack of gum in his pocket—he'd been chewing it on the plane to pop his ears. Surprisingly, he found the pack deep in his pocket and pulled out the last piece. Paul chewed for a while. Then he pressed the softened stuff to the damp spot, hoping it would hold.

Now he tested Red's cigarette lighter. It wouldn't work. The casing was dented and the wheel was bent out of shape. Well, he could forget about cooking anything or making a fire tonight to keep the animals away. He shoved it back into his pocket, thinking maybe he could fix it later. Right now he was very hungry, so he took out a strip of beef jerky. His jeans had already dried out from their dousing in the mountain stream, but for some reason the meat tasted soggy. The first taste was such a turnoff he couldn't go through with eating it, and he tossed it to the ground.

Okay, now there were no more excuses for staying perched on this branch in the middle of nowhere. It was fear that held him back, and he knew it. This was the one place that seemed to be safe, but he had to leave it. He was just climbing down to the ground when something struck the back of his neck. He heard jabbering and he looked up. There were two small monkeys following him along one of the lower branches. They were plucking some little objects from vines and throwing them at him.

Paul gazed down at his feet. Figs.

They're letting me have it with figs!

Now the monkeys were bouncing up and down and making faces at him. Paul's eyes lit up. "Okay, guys," he said, scooping up a fig. "You asked for it and you got it. Food fight!"

His first throw went wild. The second zinged between the two monkeys. One of them dropped to a one-armed dangle, grabbed another fig, and tossed it to him underhand. Paul caught it and threw it back. A third youngster, after making a flying leap to a higher branch and then doing a cartwheel down, came at him from the side.

Paul was having a marvelous time throwing and ducking, but it all ended with a nervous howl from above. That must have been Mama warning her brood against getting too close to the ground, because suddenly everything stopped. The kids hung out for a moment longer, listened to one more motherly scream, then turned around slowly and began to climb.

"So long," Paul called to them. And gathering up this unexpected breakfast, he started off in a good mood.

It wasn't long before he learned that heading downslope in the rain forest wasn't simply a matter of going down. A hill had its own bumps and dips—tough going when he had to be super-careful of what he grabbed at to break a fall or help pull himself along. And then there'd just be another, maybe slightly lower, hill to climb.

At the bottom of these jungle-covered hills he'd find water. But the streams stank and teemed with insects. Though the canteen was empty by now, he didn't dare fill it up. And since these sluggish creeks seemed to be going nowhere, it made no sense for him to follow their course.

It was probably mid-afternoon before he heard rushing water, and came out on the shore of a very narrow, clear-looking river. Again he wouldn't drink from it. The water smelled of death somewhere—something was rotting upstream, caught against a rock or a fallen branch.

But at least this stream seemed to be going places in a hurry. It was moving. And as he picked his way along the shore, Paul noticed birds flocking over a large cluster of berries.

They *had* to be filled with juice. That thought made his galloping thirst all the wilder. Paul put a berry into his mouth and carefully bit down. It was awful, so bitter he had to spit it out. Maybe these berries were good enough for the birds, but he'd rather go hungry and thirsty for a while than eat them himself. He hoped there'd be some other kind of berry further on that would be better.

Paul grew angry as he hurried along. He recalled how Orlando, the man who'd picked him up at the airport, had taken him past a market. The driver had wanted to show him all the interesting foods that were for sale there. But he wouldn't even look. He was too busy pouting. So right now he could be walking by lots of things to eat and he wouldn't even know it.

Paul decided he couldn't blame himself for what he didn't do before. That wouldn't solve anything. So he might as well just do his best to stay on the ball from here on in. If he was wondering what he could eat and drink in this rain forest, why not find out from the monkeys? *We're all from the same family, aren't we?* he thought. *Give or take a few million years!*

Yet where were those little guys now? For the next hour or so he scanned the trees as he went along and never saw or heard a monkey.

A rustling sound finally drew his gaze past some thick leaves to a slender monkey with a baby clinging to her back. Using her long tail to hold herself in place, she kept bending a vine back and forth until it snapped. Then she tipped the hollow end of it over her shoulder and into her baby's open mouth.

Paul waited until the slender monkey had gone. Then he climbed to the branch and treated himself to a long sugary sip of water. When he finished, he licked his lips just as the infant had done and smiled contentedly. This was more than just finding something to drink—as important as that was. This was having achieved a little victory for himself. Maybe even a big one. The odds of getting out of this jungle alive were beginning to look better all the time.

As he trudged along through the forest, Paul noticed a change taking place in the watercourse he'd been following. It was beginning to move more rapidly. Suddenly the stream sprang ahead wildly, and poured into another, much wider, one. The mother stream was more powerful. It had just come around a rocky bend, so nothing could be seen of where it had come from. But from further back came the roaring sound of falling water—and some of the water in front of him was still foamy white.

It smelled fresh and inviting. Paul wanted to hurry to it, but a heavy, grunting animal with a piglike snout was belly deep at the point where the two streams joined. It let loose what might have been a warning cry—and Paul realized that he'd been staring at the animal. Coming to a stop some distance off, he avoided its eyes and waited. The creature went back to its bathing, but it still seemed wary of him. When at last it stopped feeling challenged, it slowly lumbered off into the bushes.

Relieved, Paul moved down to the river. The first thing he did was pull off Red's boots, which were too roomy in the back, and shove his feet, blisters and all, into the cool water. *Oh, man, did I need this!* he thought, peeling off the rest of his clothes. These he dipped in the stream, rinsing and rubbing them until the sweat and grime were gone. He spread them out on a rock to dry. Next he smelled and tasted the water, drank a little of it, then filled his canteen and set it down.

So okay then, he told himself. He'd put first things first. Red would have said, "Good enough, boyo, yer've taken care of business like a man." Right? *Right.* And there were no crazy-looking fish around. Right? *Right.*

Slipping on his sneakers because the river-bed was filled with jagged little rocks, Paul waded deeper into the current, testing its strength. He was just considering breaking into a swim when something at his feet caught his eye—a glittering rose-colored chunk of quartz. Reaching down, he plucked the stone from the riverbed. It was beauti-ful—and back on Cape Cod that would have been reason enough for collecting it, along with fossils and seashells. But studying the jagged edge of this one, Paul's thoughts turned practical again. He wondered how he could go about working this into a cutting tool, or maybe even the edge of a fishing spear.

These thoughts were enough to delay his reacting to something else. Another sound had been added to the roar of the unseen waterfall—the throb of a helicopter.

Appearing suddenly from around the bend, it came in low. He heard his name boomed over a megaphone.

"It's all right, lad," called a voice. It was Red, leaning from an open window. "Yer folks have met our terms. Yer safe now, son. You'll be goin' home!"

Going home? Paul blinked and found himself growing teary-eyed. *I'm going home?* So it was all over. He stood there with the water flowing around his naked body. Home seemed a million miles away. Where was home? Grandpa and Grandma's house that had already been sold? The outpost where his parents worked that he'd never seen except in snapshots?

Not that Paul was thinking these questions in so many words. It was just that hearing those two words had pulled him away from where he was—naked, up to his knees in jungle river water—without putting him anywhere else.

Red was calling out something more. Through a daze, he heard it. "We're goin' to drop yer a line. Tie it under yer arms and we'll haul yer up. Do yer understand?"

Paul nodded and waved his arms. He knew clearly what was going on. He wasn't missing a thing. And that's why he noticed it right off as the helicopter's nose swung around slightly and the rope was tossed out. What he saw was the peak of a hat—like an officer's hat. The man at the controls was the Senhor!

Would the Senhor really take him back to his parents? What about what Red had told him before? "It's worse luck for yer that yer found out who the Senhor is!" the Irishman had said. There was no way the Senhor would let him live. Paul had to get to shore and make a run for it.

They were coming in closer now. The line was coming down. "My clothes!" shouted Paul. But Red didn't seem to hear him.

Waving and pointing to show what he

meant, Paul started to wade to the shore. The clothes were lying on a flat rock right in front of the wall of trees. And if he could just get close enough. . . .

Now he was almost there. Almost out of the water. Another foot or so and he could jump into the bush.

Rifle fire raked the rock in front of him, then fell back to the water. Paul leaped away to the side as the bullets churned water inches from his body. As he stumbled he saw the Tank leaning on Red's shoulder as he fired. But Red was moving, the helicopter was moving. And Paul, streaking from the water, dove like a fleeing animal into the bush.

Paul ran on and on. The insects showed no mercy to his naked body. Thorns whipped at him, tearing at his skin. And if, in his mad race to get away from the helicopter, he had disturbed the lair of any poisonous snake, his low-heeled sneakers could not have helped him. But he couldn't slow down. He couldn't watch what he was doing. He had no way of knowing whether his hunters had come down the rope after him, and that frightened him more than anything in the jungle.

The bites, scratches, scrapes, and falls were wearing him down. He was slowing, breathing hard—and even worse—feeling more out of control by the second. Finally he stopped. And when his panting died down, he listened for signs that he was being followed. Hearing none, he inspected his injuries and decided that he could not go on this way.

There was a bush nearby with leaves as wide and thick as palms. Desperately, he tore a few of them off and wrapped them around himself. While his steaming body held them in place, he used the jagged edge of the piece of quartz he'd been carrying to cut some narrow vines into lengths of rope. Once everything was tied in place, Paul made a leaf pouch for the useful rock and tied it onto a vine around his neck.

Meanwhile the jungle was rapidly growing darker. With that thick roof of leaves overhead, he could barely see the black clouds rolling in. At first everything grew still. There was a rustling sound that could have been made by a breeze, though he felt no breeze. Or it could have been made by the creatures of the jungle taking shelter from the coming storm.

But Paul decided not to look for shelter. He plodded on, letting the drenching rains cool him. Letting them protect him from enemies. Letting his cupped hands, now that he had no canteen, fill up with drinking water. But the going also got rougher. His sneakers either sucked up mud, or he stepped down on wet and rotting leaves that skidded out from under him. And Paul's body, after first welcoming the rain, soon began to chill.

Still, he plodded on downhill until beams of sunlight came through wherever an opening in the canopy appeared. The jungle was back now to its usual daytime twilight, but ahead it seemed to grow brighter. This time he heard no sound of rushing water. Was it a river or only a clearing? Splattered with mud and covered with his outfit of leaves, Paul stepped out of the rain forest.

He couldn't tell whether this was the same river as the one he'd been on before. The distance between the shores was much greater here and the water moved more slowly. Paul turned, his eyes darting this way and that to spot anything that could be dangerous.

Walking along the shore, he came to a bend. The jutting trees up ahead blocked his view of the near side of the turning river. Something that he could not see must have excited the huge black birds that were wheeling and diving there. That bothered Paul enough to slow him down. He wasn't sure, but he thought they might be vultures.

Maybe they were circling over some big dead animal. He really was in no mood to go barging in on any feast they might be having.

Moving gingerly along, he rounded the bend and saw the birds' prey. They were still circling it. They had yet to begin pecking at the eyes and the flesh. Maybe they were looking to see if there was any animal below getting ready to make a fight for the body. Or maybe a certain smell of death was needed before they closed in for a meal.

The corpse of a white man hung over the water, bent in half and dangling from a branch. And it was only because of the red-dish hair hanging straight down from the scalp that the boy recognized the Irishman. The man's face was ashen, drained of all blood. Paul had a nightmare vision of the Skeleton's long knife slitting Red's throat from ear to ear.

He gasped at the sight, then he gagged and turned away to vomit. Though his legs wob-bled under him, he started to run, but then something inside himself told him it was wrong, plain wrong to leave Red there unburied. Suppose no one had buried his grandfather, just left him out to rot somewhere? Red was a human being!

Be cool, he told himself, stopping. *You can do it. Be cool.* He turned back and, staring more often at the ground or the sky than at the man, he hauled the body down from the tree branches.

Snatches of what a minister had said over his grandfather's coffin came back to him as he heaped leaves over the body. He said them aloud. They were words like, "We commit the body of the departed," but what did they mean to Paul *really?* Nothing. He couldn't help but realize he was saying them just because they meant nothing. Just because he didn't have to really *feel* anything when he used them.

He didn't like himself for trying to keep Red's death at a distance. But what else was he supposed to do? Fall apart? Right here? Right in the middle of this jungle? Forget that! Just forget about it. Moving more quickly now, he looked for rocks to cover the leaves. He looked for bits of logs to cover the rocks. He wanted to get out of there before he started crying like a baby.

But it was too late—Paul was already crying, hard, more than he had since his grandfather died. And now—when he couldn't push away any longer the reason *why* Red had died—he began to shake. The pain of it came roaring out of his gut, filled up his chest, and exploded out of his mouth in huge sobs. At the burning center of it all was knowing—being absolutely certain—that Red must have died for trying to save *him.*

At least at his grandfather's funeral some people had tried to say a few things about him. Things that were real and true.

"All right, God, it's the truth," Paul shouted aloud, "that he killed someone in Ireland and he was running ever since! It's true that he turned into a crook who'd do anything just to make money! He was in the gang that killed the man who was only trying to drive me to my parents! And he watched a crazy guy trying to poison Indians with a hatful of tuberculosis germs and he didn't do anything to stop it! These are things he did wrong. And there must have been plenty of others. But . . . but . . . "

Wiping his streaming eyes, Paul cast around for something he could say for Red. "But my grandfather once told me that sometimes the biggest battle a man will ever have to fight is with himself. And that's what Red was doing or he wouldn't have tried to save me. Look, I don't know what I'm asking for, God. But they didn't kill him because he was just like them. They did it because he was better than them! All I'm asking is please give Red a break. Amen."

Paul wiped his eyes and walked away, feeling that there was something he'd left undone. Red wouldn't have cared much whether or not anyone bothered to say a prayer over his dead body. No, if the Irishman could say anything to him now, it would be something like, "Why are yer walkin' away in leaves? Go back and take me clothes, yer dumbo!"

That stopped Paul in his tracks. Yet the thought of digging up the body and taking off his clothes . . .

He could just picture Red cocking an eye at him. "Yer plain scared is what yer are. Whatever yer can do to save yerself, boyo, do it!"

Not happy about it, not happy about it at all, Paul turned back. It couldn't have taken him more than fifteen or twenty minutes to return. But the grave was already uncovered. The vultures were already tearing at Red's clothes and flesh.

And there were other scavengers, four-footed ones, getting ready to fight the corpse-eating birds for the remains.

Paul's eyes blurred again and he hurried off.

The grief Paul carried with him as he followed the river exhausted him more than all his running and climbing and worrying about dangers. It affected his alertness, too, and he had to remind himself several times to watch the sky for the helicopter and check for Indians in the brush. There was still some daylight left, and for all he knew the helicopter would be coming back. Paul's feet kept moving ahead, but he had no more heart for going on like this. He knew he would need to find some shelter before night came. Turning away from the river and crossing a narrower stream, Paul went deeper inland and managed to get to the top of another slope before the dimming jungle turned black.

Paul was glad this day was over. He picked a tree to sleep in and wearily pulled himself up onto the massive branches. The one he settled upon was not very wide, but he was much too tired to look for a better one. Using the last of his energy, he tied himself in safely with a vine. With his eyes still open wide, he lay there feeling empty. So empty that he even stopped believing that somehow he was going to be able to save himself.

He stared into the darkness, overtired and wide-awake. But tomorrow he'd need all of his strength. Only he didn't want to fall asleep and see Red in his dreams, horrible visions of the murdered man. He closed his eyes, hoping he wouldn't have to dream at all. All he wanted now . . . wanted . . . wa . . .

Sleep blacked out his troubled thoughts. Sleep held him in comforting arms that night the way a mother embraces a sick child. He cried in his sleep when the sad dreams came to him. Then, growing peaceful at last, Paul sank deeper and deeper into quietness.

When he awoke it was like coming back from freedom into the prison of the jungle. It was all around him, hemming him in. He had to get out of here. Had to find help! But just supposing that by some lucky miracle there was some village nearby, how—when he couldn't see more than a few feet in any direction—was he even going to find it? There was only one way to get a good look at anything, and that was to go up above the trees.

Paul stared up at the towering tree and saw that actually there were two trees. The main one had the branches. The other wound around it and had the vines. He realized now how right Red had been when he said how little Paul knew about the jungle in spite of his parents' work.

There had been many letters that were full of the wonders of the rain forest, letters Paul had only skimmed through. He vaguely remembered one in which his mother had written about "strangler" fig trees. Birds brought the seeds to the tops of other trees, and when they sprouted there, they would start to grow downward like twisting snakes until they reached the ground and sent out roots. Thinking about it now, Paul remembered that his mother said they shouldn't be called "stranglers." These trees didn't really choke off the host trees at all. They just grew with them in the opposite direction.

Be that as it may, the vines of the fig tree

could help him reach the higher branches of the other main tree—and so Paul began to climb.

On his way, he plucked breakfast figs from the trees and kept an eye out for monkeys. They were there, all right, and not at all sure what to make of him. Grave, worried-looking monkeys stared down at him as he climbed toward them.

"Hey, don't mind me, anybody," he called softly. "If I wasn't wearing these leaves and had a lot more hair, you'd see I was really a member of the family. Matter of fact my grandpa used to say that anytime he wasn't around I'd always wind up in some monkey business. But maybe that's not being fair to you guys. Truth is, you look awful serious. Like judges, you know. So I hope I'm not on trial. But if you want a confession, let me tell you about my biggest crime. Sometimes I come out with these very bad jokes. Real third-grade stuff, like knock knock jokes."

The older monkeys simply watched him climb by. A few younger ones began swinging up alongside, but at a distance.

Puffing and straining now, Paul managed a

grin. "Hi. Thanks for coming along. Wish I could do it the way you do. Of course, you don't understand a word I'm saying. But at least we're not scaring each other, right? The only trouble is I'm beginning to run out of things to say. And if I start paying any attention to how much my arms are hurting right now, I'm going to begin having real problems. So anyone want to hear a knock knock joke? I'll play both parts. Here goes:

"Knock knock.

"Who's there?

"Banana.

"Banana who?

"Okay, guys, forget the joke. But a banana would sure appeal to me right now. Get it? A peel? Hey, wait a minute! Where are you all going? Couldn't have been that bad, could it? Guess it was."

Ignored by the monkeys, he climbed in silence. There were large distances from one branch to another, and no chance to rest in between. The friction of the vines began to tear away at the leaves of his handmade clothes. The insides of his knees and forearms were rubbed raw. His palms blistered and his fingers felt as if they were losing their power to hold on. But Paul, sometimes with his eyes closed from the sting of the sweat pouring into them, drove himself on. And then—in a burst of sunlight—he was suddenly at the top.

It was like coming to the surface of an ocean. The brilliant sky dazzled him. So did the shimmering leaves. Beneath him the rain forest stretched on and on and on—first in hilly waves and then into a vast plain that was slashed by winding brown rivers.

Waiting until he grew used to the light, Paul's traveling eyes searched everywhere for man-made clearings, for buildings of any kind, for farmlands. But this part of the great rain forest seemed to be completely untouched. It was as if he were the only human being in it.

That disappointed him, sure. But right at this moment he couldn't be completely downhearted. The effort of making that climb had done something for him. He'd set out to get up here and he'd done it. And at this moment he felt like giving a Tarzan yell. And he did.

It was a moment for fun! A moment for really feeling what it was like to be King of the Apes. Grabbing a vine and pulling back on it, he swung away from the top branch toward the nearest tree below.

But he twisted around and—*Wham!*—smashed backward into hard and knobby wood. The jolt made lights burst in front of his eyes and his hands started to slide. But his legs were entangled in the vine, and when he fell they held him in place until he could reach out for another vine, free himself, and get back into the first tree. He'd gotten a nasty bump on the back of his head. Still, there was no way now that he was going to give up. Waiting until he recovered a bit, Paul experimented more carefully with short swings and less apeman make-believe. But this grown-up-type seriousness lasted only until he got the hang of things.

And then he was off, whooping along downslope from tree to tree, feeling wonderful.

Paul was discovering, as he went along, a second world of the rain forest. Way up here, above the forest floor, there were pools of rainwater in the crooks of trees. There was animal life in those pools, insects, tadpoles, frogs. And plants and flowers taking root up here that he never saw on the ground.

The hot sun of the equator had been steadily climbing in front of him all morning as he moved eastward out of the hills. Without shade to protect him from the heat, Paul was beginning to feel like a pie in an oven. His skin was starting to fry—he could tell he'd have a nasty sunburn soon. Still, he held out as long as he could.

Then a distant speck in the sky began to grow. It buzzed at first like an insect. Then it became the throbbing of an engine. And finally he saw it was a helicopter flying low, circling . . . coming his way.

Hope and fear tore at him, pulling in opposite directions. If he got down from the treetops now, there'd be no chance of his being spotted from the air. But that was just the problem! What if this wasn't the Senhor's helicopter? Maybe his parents had stopped trusting the guy. Maybe they even found someone else to go looking for him. Hiding as best as he could among the leaves, Paul waited for the craft to come nearer.

The pilot was playing this search very carefully, making large circles first, then smaller ones. His first pass of the area was much too wide. The second one was closer. And the third looked almost as if it would pass within feet of where Paul was crouching.

He trembled, but didn't move from the place. And he trembled even more when he saw who the pilot was. The Senhor. He had iron-gray hair beneath his military cap. He wore dark glasses, and his moustache curled over his hard face. The Tank was looking the other way, but the Skeleton—Paul held his breath—seemed to be staring straight at him with those glittering eyes.

But the helicopter moved on towards the nearest river. He hadn't been seen.

Probably he could have stayed in the canopy for a while longer, but he was too shaken up. And leaving the treetops of the rain forest, Paul descended into the twilight of the undergrowth.

Paul didn't really think that the Senhor had been looking for him among the treetops. No, the helicopter would be following the big river, checking out the banks, the men ready to shoot him on sight.

Okay, then—so it would be much safer to stay away from the river. But that was no good either. He needed that stream to lead him out of these hills and take him east.

Maybe the best thing was to get close to it, but not too close. Heading very carefully downslope, Paul allowed himself, just this one time, to peep at it through the trees. Not all that far above the trees, the helicopter droned and seemed to be coming nearer. Catching his breath, as if they might hear him from above, Paul crouched deeper in the foliage, not daring to move 'til it flew by. But it didn't go by. It seemed to hover in the sky overhead. Was the Senhor dropping a ladder? Were the Skeleton and the Tank climbing down to come after Paul on foot?

There he waited until long after the helicopter had gone and everything had grown still. He waited and listened for a voice, a cough, the sound of a boot in the brush. There was nothing. But maybe they *were* there, and wanted to trick him into showing where he'd hidden himself. He counted slowly to a thousand. Then he counted again. And finally he stood up to go. Paul gave all his attention to staying just close enough to the river so he could follow it—but far enough away so he could make a quick escape if the Senhor and his men came back and tried to find him by the river.

It wasn't easy. The stream wound around the last of the hills and often twisted away from him. So every now and then he had to hunt for it again, moving in just enough to catch a stray bit of sunlight. His heart was in his mouth each time, but the enemy seemed to have vanished.

As Paul walked along he noticed that the land wasn't sloping as much anymore, leaving the river to spread out in all directions. It was much shallower than before and turning into a swamp. Paul sloshed through water. His sneakers sank into thick muck. Floating leaves and rotting plants sent up a great stench. Mosquitos the size of flies and other bloodthirsty bugs circled around him, looking for ideal places to strike. Flailing his arms around, he tried to ward them off, but it did little good.

This was awful, but he had to stay close enough to the main river to find his way out of here.

Then something wiggled by him in the water. Paul jumped, but realized it was just a small water snake. But what about the big ones, like the thirty-foot anaconda his mother had taken pictures of once and sent to him? It had sprung right up out of a river to wrap itself around a deer and crush it to death. "This was the first time," she wrote, "that I ever wanted to shoot something. But your dad reminded me that our job is to help *preserve* the jungle, not to interfere with what goes on in it."

Paul shuddered at the thought of that anaconda. Was there anything here that he could use to defend himself? Wading along through the swampy muck, he spotted a floating branch. This was little more than a wide stick really, but he took it all the same. He was just stripping away the dead leaves when he saw coming at him—not a constrictor—but a crocodile! He turned to run for a tree. The muck sucked so hard at his sneakers that he couldn't move. He wrenched himself out of them, but it was too late. The crocodile opened his massive jaws—and Paul turned to face it with the stick in front of him.

He knew of course what a ridiculous attempt at a defense this was. The spiked teeth clamped down into the wood. The jaw wrenched the stick out of his smarting hands. He was defenseless, but now he'd had so many brushes with death that his system didn't react with the same terror anymore. Or if it did, he didn't feel it through the numbness that now swept over him.

But the crocodile liked that stick. Liked it so much that there was nothing else worth taking an interest in just then. Contentedly crunching, it changed course and swam on.

The numbness left Paul in an instant and he hurried away as fast as he could. And it wasn't until his bare toes smacked against slightly higher and drier ground that he remembered his sneakers. He learned within minutes what a blunder it had been to leave them behind. The roots and rocks tore at the soles of his feet and scratched his ankles. They'd be a bloody mess in a few more minutes—Paul had to find something to protect his feet.

Once again, broad thick leaves were the answer. He wrapped them around his feet, bound them with vine, and walked on. These makeshift sandals worked all right until a sharp thorn ripped through a leaf just above his right ankle and jabbed into his skin. Crying out at the sharp rush of pain, Paul quickly pulled out the thorn. To clean the wound he squeezed the skin around it, but it wouldn't bleed. So he walked on, limping slightly.

The limp didn't bother him too much as he looked for dry patches of ground to walk on. At least an hour or so must have passed before he became aware of a growing numbness in his feet and legs. It was traveling up his body, and if he could find any bright side to this, it was that he was beginning to feel lighter—almost as if he were floating. Much of his weariness was gone. And so was the growing hunger that had been making his stomach churn for so long.

Paul tried not to be terrified, tried to convince himself that this would pass. Only when he could no longer hear his breathing because it had grown so faint—and when he sensed that his heartbeat had slowed—did he gasp aloud, "I think I'm dying!" The thorn must have been poisonous.

From somewhere nearby a bird imitated his voice. "I'm dying," it squawked back, but without the same terror. "I'm dying."

Without realizing it, Paul had come to a stop. His weaving body sagged against a tree. He was starting to slide to the ground, but then the thought came to him that if he let himself fall now, he might never be able to get up again.

"Keep walking," he thought he heard the bird say. But then, that couldn't be the bird. It had sounded like Red's voice!

Red's dead! he told himself. *Wait a minute. Does that mean I'm dead too?* But then Paul pulled himself together. "I'm hearing things because I'm scared," he mumbled.

"Scared," repeated the bird.

"Can't let myself stay here."

"Stay here," said the bird.

"Screw you!" Paul screamed—and heard a flutter, but no answer.

"That's the spirit, boyo," said Red's unseen ghost. "I didn't get me throat cut to see yer give up now. Don't let that poison take over. Keep movin' or yer finished."

Pushing away from the tree, Paul ordered himself to go on. He could barely feel his legs beneath him, yet stiffly he staggered on.

He had no idea now where he was going. It almost didn't matter anyway. The point was not to stop . . . not to stop . . .

But when ferns or bushes got in the way, his pushing hands stopped feeling them. The numbness went into his wrists, hands, and arms. It grew harder and harder to make them do anything. They floated down to his sides.

"Get a hold on that stone, lad!" urged Red.

"Take it out of yer pouch."

"I can't. I can't move my arms."

"Mind over matter, son. Make yerself do it!"

Slowly, the fingers of Paul's right hand floated up like balloons to his neck, fumbled with the leaves, and brought out the jagged stone.

"Now press it, boyo! Press it 'til yer bleed. 'Til yer can feel the pain of it! And don't stop walkin'. Yer hear me?"

Paul nodded his head. And using whatever strength he had left, he made the sharp edge of that rose-colored bit of quartz bite deeply into his flesh. "I hear you, Red. Thank you for doing this for me."

"Ah, yer doin' it all by yerself, don't yer know. Yer actin' like a man."

Red's voice trailed away as Paul stumbled ahead. He called after the man but there was no answer. Perhaps that was because of the roaring in his ears.

It was an awfully familiar sound. And the feeling that went with it was of being under a wave at the ocean. For a moment he couldn't see at all, but then the wave passed over him. Looking around, Paul saw his two best friends, the twins. They were reaching the beach ahead of him. By the time he got out of the water they were already clambering up the dune to the blanket. Paul followed them, shaking the water out of his ears. They were already sprawled out and reaching for sodas in the ice chest. One of the boys pulled out an extra can for him. But Paul just shook his head and started for his bike.

"Hey, hold up, man! What's the problem?"

"I dunno. My hand's really hurting. I think I must have touched a stingray. I'd better go have somebody look at it."

"Look, it'll wear off," cried the other twin. "Hang out. We'll go back together in a little bit. You gotta be tired from that swim, man. That was a good two miles."

"Yeah, okay." Paul turned back to the blanket. He really was tired—and dying of thirst.

He was just kneeling down and reaching for that ice-cold can of soda, when the sharpest pain yet shot from his hand into his arm.

It jolted him out of the hallucination, and

straight back into reality. But Paul didn't like this reality. For a moment he actually started to sink down again into that other world. It was calling to him. His friends were calling to him. So was the ocean breeze. And the softness of that blanket. And the coldness of that soda. . . .

And death . . .

Paul shook it off and lifted his head. The storm clouds were here, the sky bursting open. He could see the rain. Water that he could barely feel ran down his face. He couldn't remember now whether it was Red or his grandpa who had said something about the hardest battle a man would ever have to face. So what was that battle? He couldn't quite remember it now. He thought about that a long, long time. And he was still trying to recall it when the rain dribbled away and stopped.

Paul thought he must have become delirious again. He was standing in front of men as naked as himself, who were painted with stripes even redder than their skin.

Three of these men stood side by side. They were leaning on long palmwood bows and talking together, but not looking at each other. They weren't looking at Paul either— in fact, they acted as if he didn't exist! But a fourth man stood a little bit apart from them, and he was certainly looking at Paul. There was a bamboo arrow fitted in his bow, which now he drew back, aiming it straight at the boy's heart. But as soon as he did so, the three men chanted something as if trying to convince him not to shoot.

He relaxed the bow and lowered the arrow. But as soon as the men started talking to each other again, he again took aim at Paul. Then the three men repeated the same chant. That seemed to convince Paul's would-be-killer, so he lowered the bow once more. But then the same thing was repeated a third and a fourth time.

Paul was beginning to understand what was taking place. They were natives of this jungle. There was a ritual going on. It was their way of mulling over what to do about this stranger.

Paul knew how important a moment this was in his life. Yet he could not help wondering about something. How was it possible to be unable to feel his own body, and yet to have his mind be so alive, so clear about everything that was going on? He was absolutely certain, for example, that if he were to have any chance of not being killed, he musn't stare into the eyes of the man with the drawn bow.

Not that Paul was feeling terrified about any of this right now. No, as a matter of fact, he was very calm. And he was curious about what the chanters were saying to talk the bowman out of shooting. Was it that this boy must be different from other white people because he came to them as naked as themselves? Well, whatever it was, Paul couldn't figure it out. His mind grew dim. He lost the last bit of control he had over himself—and his clenched right fist opened at last. The blood-covered stone fell to the ground. And a split second later Paul collapsed beside it.

The first time he awoke it was for only a few seconds . . . and only because smoke had filled his nostrils and mouth, making him cough.

When he opened his eyes there was smoke all around him, and behind that the soaring flames of a bonfire. And from somewhere nearby, though he could not see it, there was chanting and the stamping of many feet.

An Indian whose long black hair was streaked with white and whose skin looked as cracked as old leather came through the smoke to put a long, thin reed in Paul's mouth. The aged man lifted a gourd and poured something foaming through the straw-like reed.

The liquid burned Paul's mouth. It had the biterest taste he'd ever known. It made him gag as his throat fought against swallowing the brew. A hand reached out to pinch his

99

nose so that he couldn't breathe unless his mouth widened. The liquid went down, the reed was pulled away, and Paul sank back into darkness.

The next time he awakened, he was lying in a woven palm-leaf hammock in a round hut that had also been thatched out of palm leaves. He tried to get up, but his legs were so rubbery that twice he fell back. And even that small amount of effort had made his heart race as if he'd been running a marathon. Yet he couldn't help feeling joyous. He was alive! Alive! Alive! He'd thought he was dying. No! He was *sure* he was dying. But people had found him and cured him. And Paul Francis Xavier Spire was still alive!

So if it was time to rest, okay then, he'd rest. Lying back, he listened to the shouts of small children—and didn't need to understand their language to know they were playing. The voices of grown-ups gave him clues about the people he was among. He heard sounds of conversation, some friendly, some businesslike. And sounds of greeting. There was a lot of teasing going on too, especially when a man and a woman were calling to each other. (That usually made other people laugh.) And there were scolding sounds that must have been meant for children who were doing something wrong.

It seemed to Paul that these people had their personal lives out in the open in front of everyone else. That made him feel a little less nervous about being buck naked, with absolutely nothing lying around that he could use to cover himself if he went outside. Still, when he finally was able to get up and walk slowly to the door, all he did was poke his head out.

The villagers were naked too, but not completely. Some of the women had beads around their necks. A few also had loose bits of cloth over their bottoms. The men wore hoops made of straw around their waists—not that they covered anything at all down below. Still, it wasn't the same as it was with Paul. He couldn't quite figure out why—except that they all acted as if they were perfectly and properly dressed!

A number of the women were sitting on hammocks strung between some small trees in the open compound. They were busily weaving on overhead looms. A girl not much older than Paul squatted in the shade of another hut nursing a baby. Not very far from her stood a muscular young man bouncing a small child in his arms to keep it from crying. By the fire in the center of the clearing two men were turning a six-foot lizard on a spit. And close to where the lizard was being roasted, other men were using sharpened stone tools to chip flint into arrowheads.

It was the small children who noticed Paul first. They stopped their running about to stare at him out of roundish faces with eyes that were dark as night. So far they'd only seen his head, but nude or not, what was he to do? Taking a deep breath, he stepped out of the hut into the clearing around which all the other huts in the village were built.

All at once, everyone fell silent. Even the children. They all stared, and this made him feel even more embarrassed. He knew that he had to come up with something to break the tension. When he'd been lying in the hammock he'd kept hearing the playing children yell a word that sounded like *yepe* when they wanted to catch each other's attention. Not knowing what else to do now—and trying to get someone, anyone, to warm up to him—Paul called out *"yepe"* to a cluster of small kids, then grinned and waved his hand.

One of them actually started to smile back. But then a woman gave him a sharp look and the smile immediately vanished.

Paul thought somebody must have been sent to alert the rest of the villagers that he was up. Other black-haired men and women came in from a field carrying woven baskets. Some of them held tiny stalks of corn. Other baskets contained some sort of root that looked like a sweet potato. Paul remembered from his mother's letters that the Indians grew something called *mandioca*. None of the baskets were filled, however. And Paul realized that these people had stopped in the middle of their work to come and deal with him.

Nobody came near him. There must have been sixty or seventy of them, and they collected in front of the hut across from Paul's. There they waited in silence until two young men, teenagers really, returned from a nearby stream. One of them must have been the messenger—he was breathing hard from rounding up the village. The other sparkled with droplets of water, and there was still a wriggling fish on the end of his spear.

When all the tribe was gathered, someone went into the hut and came out again with, Paul assumed, a medicine man. Strung around his neck was a necklace of teeth (some of them large enough to remind Paul of his close call with the crocodile). The medicine man had a little bundle tucked under his arm. Crossing the clearing, with the tribe behind him, he held it out to the boy.

Paul realized that he was looking at a rolled-up pair of denim pants and a shirt—and before he could stop himself he flinched. It was impossible not to think of the Skeleton spitting tuberculosis germs into that hat and leaving it for an Indian to find. But the medicine man was still shoving the gift at him. How could he refuse? The pants looked a bit large and a little too long when he held them up.

He was aware that everyone was staring at him very tensely. He was aware too that the old man was making impatient movements with his arm. Were they annoyed with him because he didn't act happy about the gift? He made himself smile, but no one smiled back. Then rapidly he got into the pants first, turning them up at the bottom and pulling as tightly as he could on the belt. Now Paul gave the red T-shirt a quick once-over. For a split second he actually felt relieved to see the small bloodstain around the hole where an arrow must have gone through the pocket into the victim's heart. At least he hadn't died of some disease. The shirt itself was red and the stain had been partly washed or bleached away, but it was still a very eerie thing to put on. Memories of Red's limp body dangling from a branch over the river were flashing back to him. Fighting down a shudder, he stared at the villagers and tried to show by his gestures how appreciative he was.

They didn't seem to care one bit how he felt about the clothes. The men, the women, and even the children watched him with stony faces. With the old man standing at the front, they all studied Paul carefully and murmured among themselves. Paul sensed that it was a very dangerous moment.

But why? Weren't these the same people who had taken him in and saved his life? All of a sudden he thought he had it. It was one thing to help a stranger when he came to them a naked and helpless creature with bleeding hands and feet. But it was another when he stood before them, like a feared and hated enemy, in white man's clothing!

This was why the medicine man had him put on the pants and shirt. Now they could all take a long look at Paul and make up their minds what they really felt about him.

He looked at the man who had drawn the arrow against him—was it the day before or many days before?—and then glanced away. The man had been anxious to take no chances, and kill him from the very start. Why would he think differently now?

Maybe he wouldn't! Maybe they'd all agree with the man now that they could see Paul looking this way! He began to sweat because there wasn't a thing he could do about helping them decide. Nothing except stand there praying that they could all see into his heart in some way.

He decided to try making his mind quiet down. He didn't know why, but it just seemed right. He told himself to just stand there as silently as he possibly could and do nothing but wait. There was one, just one, reason to have hope. Perhaps these people wanted to like and trust the boy whom they had saved.

No one said a word, but as time passed the heavy mood seemed to ease up. A couple of small children began to move around. The young mother went back to nursing her child. A girl Paul's age came over to him with a gourd full of berries and wild bananas. As he reached for the fruit, the old medicine man turned away and went into his hut.

People went back to what they had been doing. The tiny village grew alive again with work, gossip, laughter, play. And Paul knew he was safe with these people.

It was several days before Paul's strength came back fully. Meanwhile he had to stay in the village recovering while most of the men went off with bows and spears to hunt and fish. The rest was for his own good, of course, but disappointing too, and he quickly grew restless. One morning he tried to slip in quietly among the women and older men when they were heading for the river. He got as far as the long canoes that were going to ferry them upriver. He had figured out they went upriver to farm, because the villagers would return with baskets of *mandioca* and other vegetables at the end of the day. But the medicine man, who didn't want to see all his good work undone, looked at his patient sternly—and Paul went back.

The older women who stayed behind spent much of their time using sharpened rocks to peel roots and grind them into meal.

But before the roots could be used to make slightly bitterish-tasting pancakes—or were thrown into a boiling pot to be brewed into a kind of beer—the meal had to be pounded and pressed with heavy stones to get rid of every last drop of its juice.

That was hard work, and the women let Paul help out. At first he was glad to be busy, but there was a problem. No sooner did they get used to him than sly looks came into their eyes and they began teasing him. He didn't need to understand their language to know what was on their minds. He got the idea well enough from their winks and laughter—and the parts of him they sometimes studied for long periods of time. They were demanding to know if he was a "man" yet and ready to marry.

Once the teasing of these women started it never let up. His blushes made them merry. They jostled each other and pointed at him and laid into him all the more. The whole thing had just the opposite effect on Paul from making him feel like a "man."

That at least was the only explanation he could give himself for doing a very dumb thing. Like a tiny kid, he obeyed a sudden impulse to stick a finger in the juice being pressed out of the *mandioca* and bring it to his mouth. A wild-eyed, shouting old woman leaped from the outdoor hammock she'd been sitting on, grabbed him by the wrist before he could taste it, and plunged his hand into a stone pot filled with water. Then she emptied the pot on the ground. The ground-up roots, it seemed, were all right for food—but only after all the poison had been taken out. After the incident, the sighing old women called him their name for child and chased him away.

The small children were delighted. Now they could have this silly bigger boy to themselves. Grabbing his hands and arms they danced away with him. Paul was glad enough to be led by these little ones and taught their games. He had all the time in the world for them, and their happiness caught on.

The little girls liked him especially. One of them made him a gift of her favorite toy—a live and beautifully colored moth. It was huge, and was tied on a cotton string. It flitted above their heads like a kite. In the heat of the next day a few adventurous children led him to a tiny waterfall. They all climbed under it, steadying themselves against a big rock while thousands of water bubbles foamed around their heads.

The water was soothing. The bubbles closing around him made everything else go away. Everything but the children. Paul's chest rose and fell. He could not remember breathing deeply in the jungle before. And for the first time in a long time he felt content. He could have stayed there forever.

Then one morning the leader of the older boys called him *yepe* and shoved a fishing spear into his hands. Grinning widely, Paul went to the banks of a swift and narrow river. Signaling him to watch, the leader stepped out on a rock near the center of the stream and began to study the life swimming beneath its surface. The others spread out along both banks and did the same.

Paul was impatient to join them, but he'd long ago learned that many things look simple until you try them. So he concentrated for a while on seeing how they crouched and held their spears, and how they thrust at the larger fish. Wanting to show the others how well he could learn, Paul was too concerned with looking and he missed several times. But when he told himself: *Forget about everything and just do it!* he lost his footing, fell in the water, and nearly broke the spear.

No one laughed at him or even smirked. He was amazed. The leader pointed to a spot next to him, and he patiently demonstrated for Paul over and over again how to spear the fish. Finally Paul managed to get a large one and the leader actually gave him a big smile for his effort. When Paul brought the big fish to the village, the old women making meal looked up from their work and seemed to congratulate him. Before parting with his comrades—his *yepes*—Paul put a hand on his chest and told them his name. They looked at him strangely as he repeated it. And as he tried to get them to tell him theirs, they stiffened up and backed away from him. Nor would anyone young or old go near him for the rest of the day. *"Yoluk,"* they muttered in fearful tones, as they did everything they could to avoid him.

Paul had no idea what he'd done wrong and there was no way to ask. Why did they look so scared when he said his name? It was almost like they thought he had done something bad, like conjure up an evil spirit. Was *yoluk* their word for evil?

He slept badly that night, and woke up screaming just before dawn, when many hands tore him from his hammock and carried him outside. At first he couldn't recognize his former *yepes* through their frightening face and body paint. Growling a fierce chant, they roughly forced him to lie back on a slab of stone—and stared down at him with glowering looks.

Oh God, he thought, *I'm a sacrifice!*

His fear must have been written all over his face. There was a roar of laughter. Then they began to paint him like themselves with berry juice. Even so, it took a while for Paul to realize that the youths were smiling at him—and that they were turning him into a warrior. In spite of their having some fun with him, this was a friendly gesture. And as soon as he got up, they shoved a bow into his hands and led him off.

Paul had no idea where they were taking him, or what he was supposed to do with his bow and arrow.

They walked through the rain forest to a small clearing just as the sun started to shine through the canopy of leaves. When the boys began shooting arrows at various things in the clearing, Paul quickly realized what this was all about—target practice! As he looked on, he realized why the leader of the boys *was* the leader. He was amazing with the bow. Paul watched in awe as the young Indian hit everything he aimed at. Eager to learn, Paul at first just studied him intently. But finally he could be patient no longer—it was *his* turn to try.

Of course he was awful. He fumbled clumsily with the bow, hardly able to fit the arrow onto the string. And all his shots were wrong, way off the mark. But Paul had never wanted to learn anything so badly. He kept at it, still shooting wildly, until the leader walked over to help him.

The two boys practiced together for hours, long after the others had left to do other things. Though they could not communicate with words, the Indian and the American understood each other. And Paul felt at the end of the day that he had made a friend— someone he could learn from.

After several days of practice, Paul began to understand the bow and arrow. And one day, he even hit a target the leader—his teacher—had just missed. It was a tense moment. Paul didn't know how his friend would take it. But after a moment of silence the boy grinned and clapped Paul on the shoulder.

For the most part, Paul felt like part of the gang now, but there was still something missing. There was some reason why his friends didn't completely accept him.

The answer came one evening when the whole village gathered in front of a hut. Following the crowd, Paul heard soft whimpering and got up on his toes to see what was happening inside. At first he couldn't understand the fuss everyone was making over a boy (who was a year or so younger than himself) being wrapped in a blanket made of soft twigs.

Suddenly the boy jolted as if hit by a bolt

of electricity. His eyelids had been pressed together, but now they flew up like snapped window shades, eyeballs bulging madly. The writhing, twisting body found no escape from whatever was being done to it. And the boy, trying desperately to keep from screaming, bit down so hard on his lower lip that it began to bleed. Paul looked at the people who were inside the hut. One of the women was wringing her hands. She had to be his mother, but she did nothing to put a stop to this. Other men and women were crowding around him, obviously praising his courage and telling him to hold on. The boy now fixed streaming eyes on a man whose arms were folded across his chest and was looking at him sternly. The whimpering ended, and the boy's shuddering grew less and less. The crowd murmured in approval.

Paul had noticed that nobody was enjoying this sight, yet everyone was watching it with fascination. Well, he didn't feel the same way about that at all! Hurrying off, he went into his tent and lay down. He tried not to think about what was going on in that other hut, but that was impossible. He knew that it wasn't an act of cruelty like the ones that Claudio, the Skeleton, enjoyed so much. This was a tribal ceremony and Paul could sense how important it was to the whole village.

Well, he was living here too, and he couldn't just ignore what was going on. Going back at last, he was just in time to see the boy being unwrapped. Well, now he knew the cause of all that agony. There were hundreds of ants—the kind whose stings had nearly driven Paul himself insane—embedded inside that blanket. The front and the back of the boy were masses of red blotches. But he was happy now and his proud father embraced him.

As the crowd began to pull away, Paul took a deep breath and went over to the leader of his friends. "Me too," he said imitating the blanket being wrapped around himself.

He had to repeat it several times before the other youth understood. *"Marake!"* exclaimed his *yepe* enthusiastically, and laid a hand on Paul's shoulder.

Later that day, Paul went into the hut of his friend. The whole tribe turned up outside and the shaman himself came to perform *marake,* the ant test. Using twigs as chopsticks, the medicine man plucked the ants one by one from a pouch and stuck them into the blanket.

It was a long wait for Paul, and it seemed almost worse than what was going to happen to him. Remembering those fiery stings, his skin began to burn and crawl just thinking about it. Still, he forced himself to keep watching and did not even flinch when the blanket was slowly brought toward him.

He could tell that the villagers approved of how he was behaving so far. But now the blanket was closing around him. And there was no way to completely prepare for the tremendous shock, heat, and pain of ants stinging him every place at once. He had promised himself not to jolt, but he could not help at least a small shudder.

Still, there was a murmur from the villagers. So far so good, they seemed to be saying. And even the leader of the *yepes,* who seemed to be acting as Paul's father, unfolded his arms and didn't look so stern.

Paul took what encouragement he could

from that, but the pain was unbearable. *I've been through this before,* he had to keep reminding himself over and over. *And this time it's happening because I want it to!*

That was the thought that kept him from shrieking, kept him still for so long that the villagers couldn't stop talking about it.

Near the end Paul almost passed out. But he had also held out. Caressing fingers soothed his fiery skin with some oily cream the shaman had squeezed from the leaves of a small plant. The leader of the *yepes* gave him a proud, approving look. Well, the ordeal was over and he was truly one of them now!

Yes—a full-fledged member of a tribe whose name, like the names of all the people in it, no one had as yet seemed willing to tell him.

It was on a day when the young men were hunting that their leader made an important gesture of friendship to Paul. Taking the boy aside from the others, he cupped a hand to his ear, looked around anxiously and whispered a word. *"Aguirre."*

Paul already knew how to say that he didn't understand. Patiently, his friend cupped a hand to his ear and whispered again. *"Yepe Paul, Yepe Aguirre. Paul. Aguirre."*

"Is that your name? Aguirre?"

Paul hadn't spoken very loudly. But the sharp-eared young Indians who had gone ahead turned back suddenly. They seemed startled and anxious. And as for Paul's friend, he had dropped his bow in panic and was staring up at the trees.

"Yoluk," one of them said unhappily. And they all murmured in agreement.

What did this mean? What was so frightening about someone's name being said aloud? Were they so afraid of separately drawing attention to themselves? And from whom? Evil spirits? Paul had guessed before that *yoluk* meant something evil. Now it seemed even more apparent that these people didn't want to anger the spirits. Didn't he once read somewhere—or was it his father who told him—that in some way or another people all over the world were superstitious?

But did it make sense, he wondered, to feel that way? Well, maybe it did and maybe it didn't. But only a few moments before, the *yepes* had been happy over their success at the hunt and full of fun. Now they plodded through the rain forest as if they thought it had become a hostile and angry place. And even to Paul—although this may just have been in his mind—it seemed that the greenish light of the rain forest had begun to dim.

Now they moved like cautious warriors. And it was not very long afterward when Aguirre, who had gone up ahead as point man, warbled a birdcall. Paul had been with the tribe long enough to know this birdcall meant *enemy coming!*

A second call meant many. The other *yepes* were uncertain what to do, but Aguirre hurried back and motioned for them to go into hiding and get ready to fight. Paul thought he understood the reason why they were staying instead of running. It was close to the village. And the enemy, whoever they might be, were headed for it.

Soon the enemy appeared. Though the intruders were silent, it wasn't because they were trying to sneak up on anyone. This was no war party. This was an entire village on the move. Some of them were limping. Others were silently weeping. Some had charred skin and terrible burns and blisters. The men were not painted for war and had no arrows fitted to their bows. They were sending their old people, children, and women ahead of them. And the most pregnant women were in front of them all. Paul, who had seen many newsclips on television of victims of great disasters, already knew what the broadcasters would call them. They were refugees.

Aguirre rose from his hiding place and went up to them. An old man, the other tribe's shaman, came up to him. Watching from a short distance, Paul saw the old man point to the sky. Lifting his skinny arms above his head, he whirled them about, and made sounds that were an eerie imitation of a helicopter.

The Senhor! thought Paul. Looking on in horror, he came to understand that the cause of the disaster was the search for him. The Skeleton and the Tank had descended on an innocent village with their modern weapons of death. Paul could imagine the Skeleton's glittering eyes as villagers screamed and warriors fell dead under rapid gunfire. He could see the flames of their huts, see them being torched one by one as the two white men ran through them looking for him.

Aguirre turned away from them and came back to Paul. The *yepes* turned to face him. *I'm going to die now,* Paul suddenly thought. *When the Senhor comes they'll show him my body! They're going to kill me!*

But no. Aguirre placed a hand on his shoulder and pointed. Paul understood. He was being told to go. To run.

"But . . . but what about all of you?" he tried to gesture.

Scowling, Aguirre pointed away again and turned his back. Paul watched him go off, leading the *yepes* and what was left of the refugee tribe, toward the village.

Paul felt as if he were being torn in half. His own instinct to survive was ordering him to flee, disappear, run! Yet at the same time this was *his* tribe now. They had cured him, trained him, adopted him. He felt safe and secure with them. Paul feared as much for the lives of his friends and their families as he did for himself.

The only way he could think of helping them was to give himself up to the killers in the helicopter the moment they showed up. It was a horror that he could barely even allow himself to think about. But secretly he followed behind the refugees all the way to the village.

From the limb of a tree, he watched Aguirre walk in ahead of them. He must have called out that there was no danger, but at first the village reacted with hostility. The women ran at the tribe with stone pots. The children screamed insults and picked up rocks. And the men, looking murderous, shook weapons in their faces. The wounded and defeated people in the middle did not answer. They stared at the ground in shame and defeat.

Then the white-haired shaman came out of his hut. Even in this heat, he was cold and had a piece of woven cotton over his shoulders. The villages fell silent as he went up to speak to the shaman of the other tribe.

Their eyes met but once, then they looked to the side and spoke to each other loudly enough for all to hear. Paul guessed they spoke of how the white men had descended from the sky with weapons, destroying the village. Faces softened. Here and there a sob was heard. And soon the refugees were being offered water and food.

None of this solved Paul's problem. Still unsure of what to do, he wandered down to the river to think. He noticed that there was something strange about one of the canoes. Usually these small lightweight boats were propped up against some tree to keep them from filling with rain water. But one of them was already lying on the shore with the paddle inside as if ready to be shoved off. Coming closer, he saw that it contained a stone ax, a bow, and a fishing spear. No two handmade weapons were ever exactly alike—and there was something familiar about these. Picking up the spear, he ran his fingers over the wood and looked closely at the hammered stone point. This, he realized, was his own. There was also a supply of wild bananas, Paul's new favorite food, on the bottom of the boat. And since the monkeys hadn't made off with them yet, they couldn't have been put there more than a few minutes before.

It had to be Aguirre who offered him this boat and put all these things here. Aguirre must have known all along that Paul hadn't left. That he'd been watching the village out of fear for them all. And this was a *yepe's* way of saying, *Go with our blessing. You are always one of us.*

Paul had learned from Red how to hide a boat from enemies in the sky. He took the same precautions now, but so far he had the river to himself. No anaconda or crocodile rose from the waters to challenge him. He was startled only once, when a harmless iguana dropped off an overhanging branch and belly-flopped into the stream. The splash shot water across the boat and washed away the sweat that was dribbling down Paul's face and into his eyes.

Still, nothing could wash away the heartache of knowing that so many others had suffered and even died in the fight he was waging to save himself. Or the fear of what might be happening this very moment back in his own village.

The rapid darkening of the sky called him back from his thoughts. For some reason, the black clouds were rolling in late today. But now that they had, the downpour was tremendous. Paul had decided ahead of time that he wasn't going to stop and take shelter. He'd keep going as long as he could and worry about bailing out the water later. But there was thunder now, great ear-shattering claps that seemed to be coming from just above his head.

Suddenly a bolt of lightning split a massive trunk in half next to the water. When the tree toppled, terror broke loose. Frogs, birds, iguanas, snakes, monkeys, and all sorts of tinier creatures—who wanted nothing more than to survive—fled their homes.

A crashing limb missed the boat, but a shaken Paul couldn't keep it from overturning. He went under. The canoe started floating away upside down, and Paul realized that at any moment it could tilt sideways and sink completely.

With lunging strokes he overtook it and threw himself across the upturned bottom to grab the far side. Pulling and falling backward at the same time, he tried to turn it right side up, but there was too much water inside.

Flailing about with his legs, he found a foothold on a rock underneath. Completely underwater now, he pressed upwards, lifting the stern above the surface with his shoulders. That didn't rid it of all the water, but it was enough to let him flip the canoe.

He bailed out a good deal more before it was possible to climb back in without sinking the boat. His paddle had floated downstream, so Paul pushed the canoe along with his hands. It was slow going, especially with the rain still pouring down into the boat. But just after the storm ended, he spotted the paddle resting among some lily pads near the opposite shore.

It was only after he'd pulled it into the boat that he realized how completely exhausted he was. At first he thought about finding some place to just get out and rest. But that would do no good. Then he'd have nothing to do but think about his village and what might already be happening back there.

"So where do yer think yer goin', boyo?" he heard himself cry out. Then it struck him as funny that he'd imitated Red. "Better grow up fast, I'm tellin' yer, lad. 'Cause there's no way of knowin' where yer bloody goin' to end up."

As he struggled to get out of his rotten mood, Paul noticed that just ahead the river poured into a kind of lagoon. The late afternoon sun slanted into it, making the water in the center dance. He didn't dare cross in the open, where he could be so easily spotted from the sky. Clinging to the shore that had the most shade he started to work his way around it. After a while he began to realize that the lake was like the palm of a hand. Five fingerlike streams ran out of it in different directions. So which should he choose? Judging from the sun, the center one was heading almost straight east. But the widest one, which he thought of as the thumb, might break out again into a large river. Only it was going south. On a hunch he took the center stream.

It turned out to be a mistake. Gradually, the narrow river dwindled into a bug-ridden swamp, full of water plants and lurking dangers he could sense but not see. Backtracking, he returned to the lagoon and paddled toward the mouth of the wider stream.

But night was coming on very quickly now. And weariness had long ago seeped into every part of his body. Maybe the best thing would be to pull over, hide the boat, and make his bed in some branch while he still had the chance to see what it looked like. Gliding the boat to a soft stop in the mud, he started to get up. But then he sank back and let his eyelids fall.

Lemme just rest here for a minute first, he told himself, and instantly fell asleep in the boat.

Paul did not awaken until long after daylight when a foot on his chest slammed him back against the bottom of the boat—and a jabbing point of sharpened stone was pressed to his throat.

14

Their eyes met with a clash. Paul's had flown wide open with alarm. But the Indian who towered over him squinted through pupils as cold and hard as two black stones. Paul didn't recognize Aguirre at first, the look on his face was so murderous. His tribal brother had suddenly become an enemy—and there could only be one reason why. The shaman had sent him!

Paul was afraid and horrified, but he also understood. The village had to be saved from the fury of the Senhor's men. And the only way to do it was by bringing the white men proof of his death.

"*Yoluk,*" Paul said softly, because he didn't know any other way to tell his friend, *I know you're not to blame for this.* In a way it was true that an evil and powerful force outside of themselves had come between them.

Aguirre acted as if he did not understand and didn't want to. He lifted the spear slightly as if to plunge it all the harder into the boy's neck. But then a grin began to spread over his face. It grew until he covered his mouth and started to giggle. Then stomping the ground, he broke into a merry dance. All at once Paul realized that this was just another big *yepe*-style practical joke, like the time he was dragged from his hammock and painted all over in berry juice.

But there had been a serious side to that first prank. And to this one, too. It seemed like the older boy still considered himself responsible for Paul's education as a warrior. And growing serious, he used a mixture of words and gestures to make Paul understand how stupid it had been to go to sleep in the rain forest unhidden or unprotected.

It took a bit longer—and a good deal of Aguirre's imitating paddling, then ducking around trees—for Paul to catch on to what the tribe had done about its problem. The villagers had taken all their belongings and gone off with the refugees into hiding. It was only after they were safely away that he was free to chase after his friend and try to guide him out of the jungle.

Paul realized what a night-and-day job it had been to catch up to him. The fleeing villagers had needed all the available boats, so Aguirre came after him on foot. But if the Indian youth was worn out, he did not let his friend see it, and insisted they shove off quickly. Paul agreed. Part of the morning was already gone and the Senhor's helicopter might soon be making another sweep. Aguirre nodded towards one of the streams that Paul hadn't even considered taking, and they set out.

As they were passing through a narrow channel, the canoe scraped against a submerged rock. Soon it sprang a leak and began to fill with water. Paul paddled while Aguirre bailed with his hands and scanned the rain forest for a particular kind of tree. Finally he pointed, and they turned in to shore.

Unfortunately, Aguirre had taken only weapons along and Paul had lost his ax when the boat overturned. The two boys scouted around until they found a rock that had a usable size and shape. Taking turns with it, they hammered into the soft wood of the slender tree until it began to drip a gummy ooze. Collecting a thick glob of it on a big leaf, they went back to the place where they had pulled the boat out of the water.

Aguirre poured the gum into the hole in the boat. After about an hour the sealant had set, and the two boys were off again in a canoe as good as new.

For the rest of the morning they traveled silently, but between these two friends there was no need to speak. They stopped only once. And while Paul gathered a meal of berries, Aguirre found a thick piece of bark he could make into a kind of paddle for himself. After that they moved along more quickly on the widening river.

But it was not very long after the sun passed overhead into the afternoon sky that they heard a helicopter drone. The nearest place to hide was a mangrove swamp. The thick roots of these trees made tangled bridges over the water. Ducking low, the boys slid into the shadows.

The helicopter circled overhead and came

in low. So low that it nearly skimmed the water. They waited until it had lifted up and gone. But no sooner had they come out than the helicopter circled back. Had that been a trick to lure them out? Had they been seen? Quickly they darted under the roots of another tree.

Once again the helicopter came in very low, and hovered over an open stretch of water. But no one fired into the mangroves. No one came down on a rope ladder. And eventually the craft lifted and flew off.

Just in case there might be another circling back, Paul and Aguirre waited until the rains came and passed. Aguirre chanted something that could have been a prayer. Paul tried to repeat it and then they set out.

Unfortunately, the sky never really cleared up after the rains. When nightfall came, the darkness swallowed them totally. They tried to move on in spite of it. And slowing down, one of them stroked the water while the other used his paddle like a blind person's cane.

But even so, the canoe snagged on reeds and water plants. More than once they had to back up, or beat their way through to some nearby place from where there came the sound of freely flowing water. So when daylight came, not even Aguirre could tell where they were.

Paul began to think about climbing a tree. But here the rain forest was so closed in that there hadn't been any room for branches to grow. Not until the very top. Climbing out of the canoe, he searched about until finally he came to the falling vines of a strangler fig. But no sooner did he lay hands on them than Aguirre came after him, shouting with alarm, "*Yoluk! Yoluk!*"

This was puzzling. What was his friend trying to tell him now about evil spirits? Maybe it was that they lived in the tops of trees and didn't like anybody to bother them. But wait a minute. That didn't make any sense when the tribe always acted as if *yoluks* were everywhere, listening in and watching whatever they did. What was wrong with climbing a tree? Paul recalled seeing children scurrying around low branches. Yes, but thinking back on it, that was only when they were in a bunch and doing it together. They would wait around to gather on the ground and then go up. They would come down together too.

Paul's eyes grew wider. Everything seemed to be coming together now. For all at once he understood why nobody in the village would ever mention his or her own personal name aloud. The evil spirits, the *yoluk*, punished anyone who dared to stand out or set himself apart.

All right then, so how could he explain to his friend that this shouldn't be a problem in his own case. He was different anyway, because his color was white.

At first, Paul drew only blank stares when he kept trying to point out the difference in their skins. But then Aguirre suddenly lit up and ran into the woods. Paul heard him thrashing about until finally he came back with a special bunch of shiny green leaves. Crushing them between stones and mashing them with water, he had Paul strip and rub the mess all over himself. When at last the naked boy had taken on the most ordinary color of the rain forest, Aguirre was delighted. No *yoluk* would ever bother to look at him now!

The climb was hard work and bruised his skin, but he made it at last. Yet Paul had overlooked the fact that this was not hill country. The trees all around him were just about the same height, so he couldn't spot any river below. What he did see was a rising column of smoke! No, more than one!

Paul was so excited as he climbed down, that he skidded and nearly fell. Those fires, he told himself, had to mean that some farmers were burning trees. Rescue might be that close!

Aguirre didn't seem at all enthusiastic when his friend spoke of fire. But he got into the boat without protest. Both boys sniffed the air as they tried to find their way through a maze of little waterways. But when the scent of smoke grew strong, Aguirre insisted that they hide the canoe and set out on foot.

There was good reason for his caution. Those were not trees that were burning, but thatched huts. Just beyond a very dense undergrowth, an Indian village was being destroyed.

They approached it, crouching. Paul was much better with arrows than spears (from all his practice with Aguirre), so he held the bow. Aguirre, as usual, led the way. Coming to a stop behind the upturned roots of a fallen tree, they gazed through the haze at the clearing in the center of the burning village. Those villagers who were still alive sat on the ground, coughing from the smoke. Mothers huddled over screaming children. Old women leaned over the dying. The men had their hands over their heads. One of them, Paul noticed, had a Mets baseball cap on his head. Could that be the same infected cap the Skeleton had left in the jungle?

The Tank slowly walked among the captured people with his assault rifle. Those squatting nearest to him cringed as he passed. They must have thought that he was choosing which of them to let live for a while and which to kill right now.

Paul's gaze swept past the village to the little field on its left where *mandioca* was grown. There, the helicopter sat like a beetle. Some twenty yards or so from its slowly rotating blade stood a man in a military uniform, the Senhor.

He acted as he were not a part of any of

this. Sunglasses protected his eyes from the smoke as he looked at the trees beyond the field. It wasn't as if he was worried about being in any kind of danger. He was too relaxed for that. Maybe he was thinking about how much money the timber around here would bring if he could find a way to get it to a sawmill. But whatever was on his mind, it was the Senhor who suddenly noticed Paul. Shouting a warning, he pointed and reached for the pistol in the holster on his hip.

But the greatest danger came from the Tank, who spun around with his AK-47 blazing. Before he could spot his target, Aguirre rushed forward, hurling the spear. Paul had no time to see where it went. The Skeleton had looked up too, his eyes feverish and grinning like a madman. His rifle fired wildly before he could even take aim. And Paul—for all his desire not to kill—let an arrow fly.

The Senhor's pistol shot fell short. But the Tank's automatic fire would have cut Paul in half if Aguirre's spear hadn't plowed into his stomach. Paul's arrow went off the mark—

but only slightly. He'd aimed for the heart; it buried itself deeply in the Skeleton's gurgling throat, instead.

The tribesmen seemed too startled at first to realize what was happening. This gave the Senhor a chance to make a dash for his helicopter. But when he stumbled and went down, they jumped up and ran for him.

Quickly he scrambled to his feet and dashed to the door of the craft. He was starting to climb in when a rock struck him in the back. Other stones kept him from getting up. The Indians closed in on him. . . .

And Paul had to cover his ears not to hear the man's screams.

It was the men and women of the village who beat the Senhor to death. But it was the freed children who ran, shouting, to where Paul stood in a daze. They formed a ring around him and talked in hushed whispers. One girl finally broke out of the ring of children and rushed up to touch him. The others joined, and they surrounded Paul with their laughter and embraces.

Their taps and touches brought Paul back from thinking about Red saying, *"I was a year older than yer when I killed me first man."* He heard a moan and looked over the children's heads. About thirty feet in front of the Tank's motionless body, Aguirre lay clutching his side. The force he'd used in throwing the spear had carried him ahead—and straight into the stray bullet that burst out of the Skeleton's rifle when it clattered to the ground.

Paul rushed to him, but Aguirre wouldn't take his hands away from his wound. An old woman hurried over. She wasted no time yanking Aguirre's hands away. There was blood, a lot of it, but it didn't look like an artery had been hit. Her own hut was a smoldering ruin, but she went into it. Poking around, she found two stone basins, one of them upside down on the other one. Still safe inside them was a small cluster of herbs. Quickly grinding them up she made a paste, came back chanting, and rubbed it into Aguirre's wound. Little by little his blood began to thicken and the flow of it slowed down.

This would help to keep him alive for a while, but the woman was at the end of her powers. There was still a bullet inside Aguirre. And for all Paul knew it might already have caused a lot of damage. Not to mention that there was a great chance of a terrible infection.

Paul's one great hope was that if he ran to the helicopter now he might be able to radio for help. But he'd thought of it too late. The furious tribe had descended on the Bird of

Death, hammering it with stones and axes. And it was only by a miracle that some clanging noise from inside it caused them all to pull back before it blew apart.

Paul ducked away, wondering, *What now?* He had to get Aguirre some medical help. Paul remembered the Indian wearing the Mets cap. The Skeleton had left that cap only a day's journey from where Paul had been kidnapped. Now Paul remembered the sound of the sawmill and the voices of men calling in Portuguese from their riverboat. He and his captors had been traveling upriver then. If he continued downriver now he'd *have* to run into someone. It might take two days to get to help, but it was Aguirre's only chance.

Paul made one desperate attempt to question the Indians about directions. They had no idea what he was trying to say, so Paul gave up and decided to go with his gut feeling—he and Aguirre would head downriver. With the help of some youngsters, Paul carried his wounded friend to the canoe.

But now the task of finding his way out seemed impossible. Going downriver wasn't so simple. There were so many twists and turns in the river, so many streams flowing in and out. At first there seemed to be no way of deciding which way to go. Several times, he came to dead ends in stagnant water, then wasted more time backing up.

In desperation Paul finally tried another tactic, closing his eyes for several seconds at a time. Maybe that might help him concentrate on hearing something—any familiar sound—that might jar his memory.

But it was the growing loss of sound that he found familiar. Signs of life were thinning out. The bird songs, the animal cries—where were they? There was only one place he'd been in the rain forest that was so empty of life and sound—that abandoned mining camp where the Senhor had picked him and his captors up in the helicopter. That camp was close to where Paul had been kidnapped, close to people who could help him. He was on the right track. Now he knew exactly where to go. He must head toward the silence.

Soon he saw the stumps of burnt-out trees, the abandoned farmers' cabins, the places where not even weeds could grow because there was no soil. The ground was nothing but rock, sand, and cracked red clay. And as Paul continued to follow these growing signs of what "civilization" had brought to the jungle, the water itself took on a sickly glow.

"*Yoluk!*" muttered Aguirre, half deliriously.

"Yup," he agreed with a sigh, thinking about what had been done to this forest by the spirit of making money at any price. "There was a big *yoluk* here, all right."

Up ahead were the miners' cast-off pans and basins. As he drew near to them, his gaze swept further on to the concrete shack up on a rise.

And at last he saw the landing strip just beyond, where a beat-up single-engine Piper Cub was perched.

Paul had screamed himself hoarse by the time he pulled in. But when the pilot emerged from the shack, it was with a revolver in his hand. Out of habit, Paul stepped out of the canoe carrying the bow, and fired a shot that zinged past the pilot's hair. The pilot gestured for him to drop it. He did so at once, but the gun stayed pointed at him while the pilot barked a question in Portuguese. When Paul didn't answer him at once, he scowled at this greenish creature in front of him and repeated his question in one of the many Indian languages.

"Look, I'm sorry but I only speak English," Paul called out. "But if you can help me I'm sure my parents can pay you."

The pilot scratched his head. "You are . . . Paul Spire?"

"Yes!"

A huge smiled broke over the man's face as he stuffed the gun in his belt. "Aha! I have found you! I have saved you!"

He came down the rise triumphantly. He jabbed a finger at the canoe. "Who is that?"

"He's my friend. He left his tribe to help me. But he's been shot and we've got to get him to a doctor."

The pilot shook his head. "No, I take you. I don't take no good-for-nothing Indian in my plane."

Paul looked at the man more closely. "But you're part Indian yourself, aren't you?"

"You watch what you say!" roared the man. "I am not same like them. I am pilot. I have children what they speak only Portuguese. I have permit for to vote. You come now or I no take you neither. And I spit on reward." He turned away. "With you or without you I go now."

Paul seemed to be thinking it over. "Okay," he said. "I have to say good-bye to him first and I'll be right with you."

"Good."

As the pilot walked off to his plane, Paul ran off in another direction. There had to be someplace he could hide. But where? He ran into a big overturned basin and ducked behind it.

Leaving his motor idling, the pilot walked back to look for him. "Hey boy, you come!" he called, but got no answer. He repeated the call. But Paul did nothing. "Too bad for you!" he finally shouted. Then with a big display of shrugging his shoulders, the pilot walked off.

But a moment later he came trotting back and headed for the canoe. "Okay, okay! He come too. Look! You see?" And he lifted Aguirre in his arms.

Paul crouched in his hiding place, ready to

run off again if need be. "I don't trust you. Take him first, then come back for me."

"You crazy? I don't come back in rains!"

"Then come back after the rains. And . . . and bring some paper from a hospital or doctor that shows you took him there!"

"You one big stinking trouble, you know that?" And grunting other insults, the pilot carried Aguirre to the plane.

After they were gone, Paul went into the shack. There was nothing in it but a few rickety old chairs, a liquor-stained wooden bar, and an old pool table with broken pockets. He managed to find a usable cue stick and a few balls. He played until long after the rains came and went.

But his thoughts were on what he had been forced to do in the burning village. So he'd beaten Red out by a year on killing a man. Wasn't that wonderful! Until now, there'd been no time to cry over it, but suddenly the tears came.

Great sobs rose up in his throat, but it just wasn't any relief to cry. What good would that do? It wouldn't bring anyone back. And if he could, would he even want to bring the Skeleton back?

He looked outside. It was too late now for his parents to come today. And so what was the holdup this time? More save-the-rain-forest business that got in the way?

He tried to shake himself out of the bad mood. He realized that there was a reason he was letting himself get so down about his folks again. Paul was afraid of how the meeting would go. Unsure of what he'd do. Or not do. It had been hard enough to play huggy-huggy with them before. But after he'd been through all this? After he'd become a killer? Well, at least someone who'd killed?

But what should he do? Hurt their feelings by shaking hands like he was meeting a couple of strangers? Should he say, "Hi there. I'm not the same little boy you think I am. But nice to see you again, anyway." That was garbage too.

There was no "right thing" to say, although he had plenty of time to think of something. Paul spent the night curled up on the floor. And it wasn't until a couple of hours after dawn that he heard the plane coming. Looking out the filthy window, he saw it touch down and roll to a stop.

Paul stepped out of the shack, squinting in the morning sun as they piled out of the plane. His mother was first, crying and laughing at the same time. Then his father, holding tightly to the pipe he no longer smoked but sometimes used as a kind of security blanket.

His mother ran wildly towards him now. His father looked happy, but almost embarrassed.

And as for Paul, he felt all sorts of things. There was love and anger and hurt and hope—and a good deal more he couldn't talk about now. And maybe not for a long time to come.

If you like **THE HOSTAGE,** you'll love
THE HURRICANE
by J.B. Watson

"Fast-moving. . . . well-written. . . . with harrow-
ing moments likely to get the reader's heart
beating faster. . . . "

—*Publishers Weekly*

And don't miss these other
exciting ***SURVIVE!*** stories:

THE BLIZZARD
by Jim O'Connor

THE RESCUE
by Jeff Morgan